DAVID'S CROSSING

BY

DONALD MORRISON

Published by Dark Forest Publishing

ISBN- 9798988114116

BISAC: Fiction / Thriller / Adventure

First Edition

Printed in the United States of America

This one's for me.

Chapter 1

"All right, Carol, I'll catch you tomorrow."

Michael Connor, or Mike as he preferred, walked across the parking lot, the soft soles of his shoes squishing against the cement. The smell of diner food and grease wafted behind as a remnant of his last eight hours. His once white apron dangled limply at his side like a crumpled tartan of time and service, the cloth soiled with all the colors of a lunchtime diner menu. Glorious smears of greens, reds, browns and black painted the fabric he carried in his hand in faded and fresh stains. A single strand fell loose, dragging on the ground beneath. Mike took no notice.

Behind him a waitress in her late forties pulled away the cigarette she was holding to her lips. In a puff of smoke, she called out, "Have a good night, Mike. And tell the missus I said hello."

"Will do, Carol."

Mike lifted his keys out of his pocket, jingling through them until he found the large plastic-handled one with which he fumbled and twisted into the lock. With a creak, the heavy steel door of the old Town & Country station wagon screeched open. The smell of sun-worn dashboard plastic and faded cloth drifted out to meet him. He tossed the apron carelessly into the back seat and settled heavily behind the wheel.

For the next few minutes Mike sat and enjoyed the worn seat. The soft jab of a loose spring digging into his backside went nearly unnoticed as he decompressed. He sat there with his head leaned back, gaze locked to the streetlight across the lot. A warm tingle worked its way up from his feet and spread to his legs. The silence passed as he let the day's work fall away. Then he took a single deep breath, exhaled in a heavy gust and reached out, pulling the door closed with a solid *thump*. He allowed another moment to pass before he leaned forward and turned the key in the ignition. Mike's motions were ritual. He'd been cooking at the same diner for the last six years, and every time he got into his car he felt the same warmth of relief. He liked his job. He found a shameless comfort in it. He'd always enjoyed cooking and it provided well enough for his family—alongside his wife's income, anyways. But he still felt that relieving satisfaction every time he got into his old station wagon at the end of a shift; though fleeting, since he would be back the following day. Tonight was no different, however he did begin to feel a little more anxious with Christmas just around the corner. With that last thought he put his vehicle into reverse, backed out and began the short drive home.

Chapter 2

The wagon turned left off the main road. A low crunching came from its tires as they pushed through the thin layer of gravel running across the entrance to the lane leading back to where he lived. Their home rested on one of six lanes, all lined with similar style mobile homes in the community he and his wife, Cheryl, had purchased seven years ago. They'd wanted to buy a house, and for five years prior to that had discussed it countless times. They were just waiting until Cheryl finished her nursing degree and he was able to move up to management. But then David happened, an unexpected blessing. "*A fortunate accident*," Mike would also say, but only with his close friends. They hadn't been trying to get pregnant; "*One in a million chance*," the doctor had said. "*Birth control has a ninety-nine percent effectiveness. It looks like your boy's that one percent*." And with that they were a family. Seven months later David had been born, happy and healthy.

That was also when he and Cheryl realized that they weren't going to be able to wait for things to fall into place, and the single apartment they were living in at the time wasn't going to work for much longer. So, they found themselves quickly navigating their options, coming to realize that for what they would spend on a downpayment for a house, they could fully purchase a mobile home. It wasn't exactly what either of them wanted, far from it, but it had two bedrooms, a bathroom, and a small yard where David could play, so they took it. And now, as Mike drove his car up the lane towards the trailer stationed second from last at the end, he reminded himself that it wasn't that bad. It wasn't the house they'd always fantasized about, but it was paid for and it was theirs.

As Mike pulled into the parking space, his eyes scanned outside of the window while the car rolled to a stop. He did this every night without thinking, the action as automatic as it was unintentional. There were three things Mike looked for as he shifted the car into park. First was the light in David's room. He searched for the tell-tale flicker on the ceiling that indicated if David was locked away playing video games again. Next, he looked for the same flicker in the living room. That would tell him how quiet he needed to be when making his entrance. Sometimes Cheryl went to bed early. She had enrolled back into nursing school now that David was old enough to ride the bus to his school in the mornings. Getting back into the routine of nightly homework with their son left her exhausted at times.

Mike's lips pulled into a smile as he spied the familiar flutters of light in the living room. Cheryl was still up watching TV. The third thing he looked for was how many cars were crammed into the parking space and accompanying yard of the trailer opposite theirs. A redneck asshole and his girlfriend lived in that trailer, and more often than not they had a dozen of their redneck friends over drinking and blasting country music into all hours of the night. Mike had no issues calling the police because of the noise and occasional fights. You could imagine the wilting friendship that had birthed between them from that. When they did see each other, Mike was normally greeted with a middle finger, and that was if the asshole was feeling particularly polite that day. Tonight however, it was luckily just the one truck. So, Mike reached out and turned his car off, sitting in silence as the engine clicked a few times. Then he put on his best *it's been an amazing day at work* look and made his way inside.

"Hey babe," he greeted, stepping in and closing the door behind him.

His wife looked up from the couch, its tan fabric bright against the soft brown of her curls dancing across her shoulders as she turned to smile at him. Mike was instantly reminded of how very much in love with her he still was.

"Hey hon," she replied, not taking her eyes off him. "How was work?"

Mike made his way over, leaning down and pausing just inches away to study her every feature.

"What?" she asked behind a squint. "Weirdo."

Mike smiled. "You're beautiful."

"Aw," she smiled as a flush moved across her cheeks. "Thank you."

He leaned forward and kissed her softly.

"How's the boy?" he asked. He pulled back and started walking towards the kitchen.

"I asked you first," she shot back, matter-of-factly. "He's good. Playing his video games."

"Work was good," he answered, pulling the fridge door open. The kitchen illuminated with a dull glow. Mike pulled a bottle of beer from within, closed the door and twisted the top off before taking a long sip. "I'm guessing Jim's got some family in town or something," he continued, not moving from his spot. "He asked me if I could cover him Monday."

"Monday?" Her reply was covered with an apprehensive surprise. "Wow. Really?"

Mike scoffed, his eyebrows drawing closer together for a moment. Then he reached up and lightly scratched the top of his head. "Yeah. I told him Monday's bowling night. Ain't missed it in five years, not about to start now…"

Cheryl smirked, her eyes narrowing. "Yeah. I know. You put our anniversary on hold when it falls on a Monday."

"Hey. I have one night a week that's mine. The rest of my life is yours."

"That is terrible! And awkwardly sweet... I think."

"Awkwardly sweet," Mike smiled, eliciting the same from her. "Okay."

"Better stay that way."

"For my sake."

"At least you've learned," she grinned.

"I ran into George from the video store today." Mike took another pull from his bottle.

"Oh. How's he doing?"

"He's good. Opinionated as always."

"What was his opinion today?" Cheryl grinned, already seeing where this was leading.

"Well. George, in his infinite wisdom, apparently thinks we should go to Chambers to get our tree. He says that's what *normal* folks are doing."

Exaggerated shock and appall washed across Cheryl's face. "And give up the opportunity to go freeze our butts off in the woods walking around while we get all wet and muddy? Why in the world would we ever wanna give that up? How could we live with ourselves not having the absolute pleasure of carrying a wet, snow-covered tree five miles through the woods back to the car?"

Mike smirked at her sarcasm.

"We're going to get the tree?!"

Mike and Cheryl both turned to the hallway to see their son come strolling out, his Transformer pajamas hanging loosely around his small frame. Mike turned his gaze back to Cheryl and lifted his beer in a toast. "And there you go," he smiled. "That right there is exactly why."

"You suck," she smirked, folding her arms in a dramatic motion across her chest.

"Hey dad," David said, stepping into the room.

"And how was your day?" Mike asked, watching as David bee-lined for the fridge.

"You know."

"Oh," Mike replied, giving Cheryl a look of surprise. "I suppose I do…" He smirked and shook his head with a smile.

Behind him David pulled the fridge door open and grabbed a can of soda from within, cracking it and taking a sip before closing the door. In that instant Mike thought he captured a little bit of himself in the boy's movements. A thin smile pulled at his lips.

"Don't you think it's a little late for that?" Cheryl asked, realizing why David had opened the soda *before* turning around.

"Eh," David replied with a sheepish shrug.

"Okay…"

"So, I was thinking, how's Saturday sound?" Mike asked, his question offered to both. "Weather report says it shouldn't be snowing."

"Awesome!" David barked, brimming with excitement.

Cheryl looked past Mike to her son. "You really enjoy going all the way out to the woods to cut down a tree?"

"Yeah! It's tradition."

Unseen by him, Mike smiled widely at his son's words, raising his eyebrows to his wife who squinted back with an unheard grumble.

"All my friend's parents just go to Chambers to buy it," David continued. "It's super cool that we actually get to go out and pick the exact tree we want. Way cooler than just going to buy one. That's lame."

"Okay," Mike smiled, turning and brushing his hand through his boy's hair. "Well how about you go get washed up. I gotta do some *convincing* with your mom." He paused, smiling again as she shook her head in defeat. "Go on," he added. "Dinner'll be ready in just a bit."

"Okay dad," David sounded, turning and making his way towards the hallway.

As he passed the couch Cheryl reached out and snatched the soda from his hand. "You can have the rest with your dinner."

David let out a small resigned gust of air. "Fine…" He continued down the hall, disappearing into the bathroom and closing the door behind him.

Mike took another sip from his bottle and smiled.

"You're terrible," Cheryl smirked. "Both of you."

"Hey," Mike grinned. "I can't help it if I have good genes."

His wife sighed, a small grin nearly escaping as she turned her attention back to the television.

Chapter 3

"How was Scouts today?" Mike asked. He scooped a small portion of mashed potatoes onto his plate before setting the serving bowl back down. David cut into a piece of the chicken that Mike had reheated for them.

"It was good," David replied. Mike waited for more; food poised on his fork for a continuation that wouldn't come on its own. He smiled slightly.

"Just good... That's it?"

"Well," David added, his mouth full of food, "Jerry got his firearms badge."

"Oh," Mike nodded, immediately glancing at his wife and waiting for what was to follow.

"Do you think I'm old enough to get mine yet?" David asked as if on cue.

Mike navigated carefully around the question. It wasn't something he had an issue with, but Cheryl wasn't too fond of guns. It was a conversation he'd breached with her once before that had ended in a stalemate.

"You've already got six. How many more do you need?" He paused, watching briefly for a reaction. "I mean. Do you even still have room on your vest?"

David set his fork down, lifting up his hands as he began to count them off. "I've got camping, lifesaving, first aid, hiking, backpacking, chess, climbing, exploration and fishing." He paused while silently doing the math in his head. "That's nine."

"Oh," Mike replied, realizing his error. "You have nine. I'm sorry."

"Tommy Jenkins has fifteen," David countered immediately.

"Well, I guess you better get to tying them knots then."

"Mike!" Cheryl snapped across the table.

"I'm just playing with the boy," he defended. He refocused on his son. "Look. This summer we'll get you all caught up. We'll make Tommy Jenkins look like a Cub Scout, how's that?"

David smiled. It was his first year as a Boy Scout, and he was trying to keep up. Everyone else's parents had the money to buy them their bows and arrows, BB guns, and everything else they needed to get all their badges. He knew his parents weren't rich. His dad didn't make a lot of money working at the diner and his mom had just started working again; so he didn't make a big deal about it. But he still didn't want Tommy Jenkins to get all of his badges first. David didn't like Tommy too much. He was kind of snotty.

"Okay dad," he replied, lifting his fork back up. "Promise?"

Mike gave him really big smile, holding his hand up and making the Scout symbol. "Scout's honor."

This elicited an equally large smile from David, who shoved the loaded fork into his mouth happily.

Mike lifted his second beer, taking a sip and then setting it down. "So, I was thinking," he said, winking at Cheryl before turning his gaze back to David. "With you being a Boy Scout now and all, maybe you'd wanna be the one to pick the tree this year?"

David almost spit out his food, nearly choking while trying to swallow the entire bit down. His eyes widened.

"Really!?"

"I mean, unless you don't want to. I'd understand—"

"NO!" David interrupted fervently. "I'd love to! Thanks Dad!"

He pushed his chair out and stepped over, wrapping his arms around Mike in a large hug. Mike shared a loving smile with his wife as he gave his son a squeeze.

"Wasn't there something you wanted to tell your dad?" Cheryl asked, looking to David.

"Oh!" David said, pulling back. "So, there's this new game that just came out and Kyle from school said it's really cool. Way cooler than Mega Man."

"Oh, it is, is it?" Mike asked, glancing back to Cheryl as he played ignorant to his son's present suggestion.

"Yeah! It's the new Zelda game. And I was just thinking, you know… with Christmas coming…"

"You want a new video game, is that what you're asking?"

"Well…"

"Maybe you should ask Santa for it?" Cheryl suggested with a smile.

"Santa's not real."

"Ouch!"

Mike laughed, lifting his beer in a toast. "And here's to the last of our son's childhood."

"And who told you that?" Cheryl asked, feigning shock.

"Mom. I'm ten. Everyone knows Santa isn't real."

"Jeez," she replied, her brow furrowing. "Sorry for trying to keep the magic of childhood going for you."

"I'm not a kid anymore, Mom," David responded flatly.

Now Cheryl laughed.

"You hear that Cheryl," Mike remarked with a smile. "Boy's already prepping for his teens. You ready?"

"God…"

"Look Kiddo," Mike said, turning his attention back to David. "Why don't you go ahead and put your dishes in the sink, wash up and get ready for bed? We can continue your Christmas request list when you get home from school tomorrow."

David accepted the terms with an easy, "Okay." He scooted his chair out and picked up his plate, turning and making his way to the sink. He didn't see the smile or amused looks shared by his parents behind him, nor the soft shake of his mother's head as she replayed his words in her mind. He did realize that he was sleepy, and it was already late. So, he set his plate and cup in the sink and ran a bit of water over them before turning and making his way towards his room.

Chapter 4

Mike stepped out of the local hardware store, the sound of the small brass bell above the door still ringing behind him. There was a heavy chill in the air and scattered flakes of snow drifted down around him. As he made his way towards his car, he found himself once again admiring the small-town serenity.

"Hey Mike!"

In that same moment, he was reminded of another one of the small-town facets. Mike turned to face the older man. Jack was gruff around the edges with a little bit of country still clinging to him in faded wrangler overalls and a worn flannel jacket. Mike exhaled, watching the cloud billow outwards. "Hey Jack. How's it going?"

"It's going," Jack replied as he closed the space between them, his gaze drifting to the large spool of twine Mike held loosely in his grasp, the receipt wrapped snugly around it. "Still dragging the family out into the freezing middle of nowhere to cut the old tree?"

Mike felt the insinuating jab and found himself wishing that he had dropped his keys, fumbled with his change, or decided to check the tool section. Anything that would have placed him just a few minutes later coming out.

"It's tradition," he replied, shrugging it off both literally and figuratively.

"Why you go through all that trouble I'll never know."

Again, small-town judgment came delivered in a thin wrapping of condescendence. Mike bobbed his head. He knew the other man didn't mean to be rude, it was just how he was. Jack was friendly once you got to know him. He and his wife had been one of the first to go out of their way to welcome them to town. It had only been a few weeks after he and Cheryl had settled in that Jack had offered them to join him and his wife at the diner for breakfast. They were older, set in their ways, and didn't take too kindly to the new technologies. They pretty much hated anything that represented the "big city," but had somehow taken a liking to him and Cheryl. So, over time they had learned to carefully navigate conversations with the couple, making doubly sure to avoid bringing up religion or politics. Mike had once made that slip over a few beers... He wouldn't be doing that again.

"Still don't understand why ya'll don't just go to Chambers. They're just as fresh."

Mike smiled. "Been doing this so long, I think buying a tree just wouldn't feel right, Jack."

"Fair enough, I guess." Jack paused, lifting his gaze up to the flakes which were beginning to fall a little heavier. "You still going to the same area off the old 95?"

Mike grinned again. "You know it. Best trees in the county are off that old logging road."

This got a chuckle out of the older man. "You know, I'd probably give it a try myself if it wasn't for these old bones freezing up in the winter. That and it's hard enough just getting Mavis to go out for groceries when it's under fifty out. Couldn't imagine trying to get her to traipse through the snow looking for a tree. I'd never hear the end of it."

Mike nodded with a smirk. "Yeah, I can imagine that."

"Speaking of our better halves, how's yours doing?"

"Cheryl? She's fine—just joined one of those *ladies' clubs*, quilting and what not. It's good for her though, gets her outta the house."

"That's good. And what about the boy?"

"He's growing. Probably gonna be taller than me by next summer."

"That's what they do."

Mike took that moment to glance up at the falling white and then to the parking lot. "Speaking of David, I gotta get going. Need to pick him up from his Scouts meeting." He paused, watching as Jack nodded with a slight smirk. "Good running into you, Jack."

"Mm," Jack replied in an approving grunt. "Same to you." He paused, a more serious tone weaving into his words. "See you at the lanes Monday?"

"You know it," Mike replied. "I might even be able to make up for the lousy games I rolled last week."

"Oof," Jack recounted. "Two seven-ten splits in a row…" He shook his head, releasing a long breath. It billowed out in front of him where it hovered a moment before dissipating upwards.

"Thanks for reminding me."

This time Jack grinned, his lips pulling back to expose the tobacco and coffee-colored row of teeth. "Can't let you forget. Don't want you goin' and getting all cocky now," he chuckled, sticking his hand out to shake. "You have a good one."

Mike reached out, grasping the rough hand in his own and shaking. "You too, Jack." He pulled back and turned, starting towards his car. "Send Mavis our regards."

"Will do," Jack called out over his shoulder with a backwards wave.

Mike continued towards the station wagon.

The flakes were falling thicker now, but the ground was still too warm from the sun's heat earlier in the day. None of it was sticking. Still, the ground was saturated, and the thought of black ice flickered past Mike's mind as he reached out to open his car door. It was at least another week or two until they needed chains, but since they were headed out into the rough, he figured he'd get them on a little sooner. He made mental note and grasped the cold metal handle.

Mike slid inside and closed the door, reaching out to stick the key in the ignition. He immediately flipped the heater to high as soon as he turned over the engine. The warmth took some time and he shuddered off the cold while waiting for the engine idle to steady out before putting the car into reverse and backing out. Mike knew that by tonight there would likely be six inches of snow on the ground; by morning likely a foot, and as he pulled onto the main road he went through his mental checklist. Tire chains, hand saw, twine, heat blanket and extra food just in case. All secured. He loved the adventure of cutting their tree, but he also knew the dangers that could come with it. The last thing he wanted was his family being stuck out in the woods for two days while he walked back to town for help. He knew that would be the end of the tradition if that happened, and though Cheryl pretended not to like it, he knew that the moment they got out there and she was surrounded by miles of pristine nature and endless forest she would get a look on her face that was yet another reminder of how much he loved her. It was another reason he lamented the thought of ever buying a tree.

Overhead the sky grew darker and darker, the clouds lowering closer to the ground as they billowed grey and white. The temperature dropped steadily and people began wrapping up for the day and making their way home.

Chapter 5

David was standing under the awning of the local Elks Lodge, one of three boys dressed in their blue and yellow uniforms. Youthful excitement swarmed around them and all were trying to get in as many words as possible before their respective rides showed up and they were whisked away. Their meetings were only an hour long, and they had to manage fitting a week's worth of conversation in the twenty minutes following.

"...and Tommy's already talking about his *next* badge..."

"Whatever," another of the boys replied, his face scrunching up. "Just cause his parents are rich and can buy him whatever he needs to get it..."

David looked past as the boy in question stepped into a sleek black car. Brands meant nothing to him and he wouldn't have known the difference between a Civic and S Series, but he did know that when your parents could afford to send someone to pick you up, that that meant you were rich.

He pulled his attention back to the others. "I think I've finally convinced my dad to let me get my firearms badge."

"Wow!" one of the others exclaimed. "You think he could help me get mine?"

"Ask your mom. I think he would."

"I want my archery badge," the other boy added. "Not even Tommy has that one yet."

"Don't say that too loud," the first boy replied. "His mom might hear you and go buy him a bow and arrow."

There was a shared chuckle between them, though they all knew he was probably right. Tommy always got what he wanted.

"I wish my parents were rich," the other boy sighed.

David's attention was pulled away by the sound of his dad's engine pulling around the corner.

"Looks like your spaceship is here," the first boy smiled.

"See you next week!" David responded, turning with a wave and starting towards where his dad was pulling to a stop.

"Hey guys," Mike called out as David opened the door.

"Hi Mr. Connor," the other two shouted back as David slid inside, shutting the door and giving one final wave.

"So," Mike asked before putting the car in gear. "How was your meeting?"

"It was okay."

"Okay..." Mike smirked. "All right."

He put the car in gear and started off.

"Anything interesting happen?"

"No," David replied, his gaze falling out the window. The next few moments passed in silence.

"Tommy got his canoeing badge," David finally said, breaking the pressing quiet in the car. "I hate it," he sneered. "He always gets what he wants because his parents are rich. It sucks."

Beside him, Mike took a deep breath and let it out slowly. He'd seen this conversation coming for some time.

"I'm sure his parents worked really hard to get where they are. That's not Tommy's fault."

"But they didn't," David replied, turning to his dad. "His grandpa was rich, they just inherenced it."

"Inherited," Mike corrected casually. "And well. Some people are just lucky."

David scoffed, shaking his head, and returned his gaze out the window to the snow beginning to layer the park they were driving past.

"But hey," Mike added in his attempt to make his son feel better. "I bet stupid Tommy doesn't get to go out and cut his own Christmas tree, does he?"

David lightly shook his head back and forth, the anger he'd welled up gently deflating. "No. They probably go to Chambers." He paused, turning back to his dad. "So lame."

"Right!" Mike agreed with a glance as he reached out and rested his hand on David's leg. "See. Tommy Jenkins doesn't have everything."

"Almost," David retorted.

"Remember. Just because you have money, doesn't mean you're rich. There are different kinds of rich."

David nodded, trying to understand.

"So, I was thinking," Mike added a few moments later. "There's gotta be a way you can catch up to Tommy without having to wait for summer. I stole a look at your guide. Hope you don't mind." He paused, waiting for a reply that didn't come. "You know, there's actually some merits in there that I might be able to help you get."

David turned to him, excitement renewed. "Really!? Like which ones?"

"Well. Cooking for one." Mike paused. "I think I could sneak you in one morning when you don't have school and show you some things at the restaurant." He paused again, mind whirring with prospects. "And with your mom back in school she has access to the observatory, so we could get you your astronomy badge. I also think that if you happen to be wearing your backpack when we go get the tree, wouldn't that count for that one?"

David smiled, nodding in agreement.

"You could help me change the alternator on this old girl when we get back, too. That's your automotive."

"Thanks dad," David replied, the warmth in him not just coming from the blasting heater.

"I wonder what Tommy's gonna say when you get ten merit badges all at once. I bet that's something his parents couldn't buy."

David nodded with a large grin. "Man. He's gonna be mad."

"Good," Mike replied. "But let's just not tell your mother *why* we're doing this yeah?"

"Okay."

"Good. I'm glad we have an understanding. Now why don't we spent the next couple weeks showing that Tommy jerk how Boy Scouting is done?" Mike stuck his hand out, balling it into a fist. David looked over to him, the smile on his face growing. He then balled his fist and bumped it against his dad's. All of the sudden he didn't feel so bad. The sadness faded away like the fog on the glass beside him. Along with the excitement that now filled him came the courage to ask a question he'd been tiptoeing around for weeks.

"Dad," he started.

"Yeah?" Mike replied, hearing the certain tone that meant something bigger was following.

"I know you think I'm still too young, but I really wanna get my firearms badge. It's the one badge that Tommy's mom won't let him get. And you have your rifle." He paused, his dad sitting beside him waiting for the inevitable conclusion to the question. "I was thinking, maybe you could at least start showing me some safety or something?"

Mike took the next few breaths in silent contemplation. He knew the effects his response would have, either from David or from Cheryl depending on which it was. He prepared the carefully calculated answer he'd had a few weeks to contemplate.

"Look," he began, his brow furrowing lightly as he watched the road ahead. "It's not that I think you're too young. It's just... Guns are dangerous. They're not toys—"

"I know dad!"

"I'm not done," Mike said shortly. Again, a thick silence fell between them. Mike exhaled sharply. "I just don't want anything to happen to you, that's all. We love you very much, son, and neither your mom or me want you to get hurt." He paused, seeing the defeat working back across his son's face. "But with that said... I also know how much getting that badge means to you. So, here's the deal."

David faced him, his face illuminated with gleeful anticipation.

"I'll help you get that merit badge—"

"YES!" David blurted loudly.

"I'm not done," Mike repeated sternly.

"Okay dad," David was quick to reply, slinking back. "Anything."

"Look. If you can keep your grades up for the rest of the year, and you don't get one C or D, then this summer, when the snow finally melts, I'll take you out to the range and teach you how to shoot."

"Thank you!" David exploded, lunging across the bench seat to wrap his arms around Mike.

"Alright now," Mike smiled, patting him on the shoulder. "Don't get us into an accident."

David pulled back. "Thank you, Dad."

The genuine sentiment in his words brought a tickle to Mike's eye and a flutter in his chest.

"Man," David whispered a few moments later. "Tommy's gonna be so jealous..."

Mike smiled, basking in the feeling. He knew, however, that it was going to be short lived because the moment he told his wife that he had caved in and agreed to it, he was going to have an entirely different type of conversation; one that wouldn't end with him feeling warm and cuddly. But that was later, and this was now. He wanted to enjoy this feeling for as long as he could, so he let his gaze fall back to the road and enjoyed the cheerful silence of the ride the rest of the way home.

Chapter 6

A heavy cold had worked its way into the air, carried down from the mountain on snow-chilled breath. The heater in the wagon was topped out at eighty and what remained of the ice not scraped away that morning clung tightly outside. Dance music played loudly, the college DJ spinning the hottest new tracks as Mike made his way through town to the local tire center. *"Time to chain her up,"* he'd said with a chuckle before leaving that morning. They'd only gotten a few inches of snow the night prior, much less than he had anticipated, and most of that had already been cleared to the side of the road by the early morning plows. But there were no plows where they were going, and he wasn't going to risk getting stuck on a dirt road with his tires spinning. Again, he loved their tradition, but he knew even Cheryl had her limits.

"And there's another absolute fire set by DJ Evan-D. You're listening to KSUU, Thunder 91."

Mike reached out, turning the radio off as another long set of commercials started up. Outside a string of closed shops drifted past. It was still early and most of the town's shops didn't open up until around nine, save for Chambers and the local diner he and Cheryl used to frequent before David's birth and the cabin fund. He passed through the next few intersections, lost in a daydream, thinking about the coming holiday and wondering if Cheryl was going to like the necklace and earring set he had sitting on layaway. Just ahead one of the stoplights had gone out and a police officer stood in the middle, bundled and cold as he directed traffic.

Mike pulled up, slowing down as he rolled his window down. "You guys really need to get that thing fixed," he called out, eliciting a small chuckle from the officer.

"I'm getting paid by the hour," the officer smiled back.

Mike checked his rearview, no cars behind.

"I didn't see y'alls name on the tournament roster," Mike said, bringing his car to a stop. "'Fraid we'd knock you out again?"

The officer's name was Blake and he was the captain of the Ten Pins, another bowling team that played on the leagues, and close rivals with his own.

"Ugh," Officer Blake called out, a cloud billowing outward just above his scarf. "Yeah. "We're gonna have to sit this one out this year. Jerry just had knee surgery and Jeff's planned some trip to Italy or someplace like that." He paused, shrugging nonchalantly. "Guess you guys are lucky this year."

Mike laughed. "After that one-forty you threw the other day, I'd say you were the one that's lucky."

"Yeah," Officer Blake replied. "Don't remind me." He paused, glancing behind him. "Where you off to this early?"

"Gotta chain this girl up," Mike answered, smiling as his joke once again tickled him. Heading out to grab our tree tomorrow. Don't wanna find myself stranded with the family on that old logging road. Pretty sure Cheryl'd skin me alive."

"Yeah. Best to avoid that."

"Yep," Mike replied. "Well. Best let you get on with it. Looks like you got your hands full."

The officer shook his head with a smile. "Mind the speed limit, a lot of traffic this morning."

Mike laughed, tipping a finger to his forehead as he pulled away. He rolled his window up and reached out, flipping the radio back on long enough to hear another commercial spouting away. He turned it back off and continued on.

Twenty minutes later he was sitting in the waiting room of the tire shop, flipping through an old issue of Popular Mechanics while they added the chains to his tires.

Chapter 7

David sat in class, his eyes wandering up to the clock on the wall. Two thirty-five. Only another twenty-five minutes until he was free. The teacher droned on from the front about the importance of finding a strong career and how everyone needed to go to college. David only heard bits and pieces, enough to be able to answer any questions should they come his way. The subjects they were learning bored him. He'd heard his mom say something about A.D.D. He didn't know what that was, but she had said it meant he was too smart for the things they were teaching and that he needed to have more of a challenge. He didn't know about that, but he did know that he oftentimes found himself bored, or just drifting off, thinking about things and fantasizing about life and imagined situations.

He pulled his gaze from the clock, letting it dance to the window for a moment before pulling it back. As he did his eyes settled on the girl sitting three chairs in front of him. Brooke. She was a new girl. Her family had just moved to town from California. Brooke had dark brown hair, the prettiest smile, and eyes that made him feel something he never had before, something he didn't quite understand. Some of the other boys had immediately latched on and teased him when he had got caught staring one day. He let his gaze linger for a moment longer, the strange thought moving through his head. *I bet her hair smells really nice...*

"So, what benefits do you think that would have? David?"

David pulled his gaze away, moving it to the teacher at the front of the class. He'd been loosely following along. "Um. It would make it easier to get a good job?"

"Yes. And what would that do?"

"It would let you get more money?"

"Exactly," his teacher confirmed, continuing on to the rest of the class.

David let his gaze wander back to the window. The sky overhead was a light grey and the mountain behind was hidden from view. His mind drifted to Scouts and he found himself remembering a camping trip the prior summer when his parents had taken him to a place called Monument Valley. They had camped there for four days and he had spent that time tracking small animals, catching lizards and climbing up massive boulders. On one occasion he'd gotten yelled at by his mom for attempting to climb a really steep hillside and making it about halfway up before getting stuck. It had taken his dad almost twenty minutes to get to him down and the memory brought with it the same flush of embarrassment he had felt then. What he'd liked the most about that trip was that his parents had let him build his own structure out of branches and fallen debris. It was sturdy and big enough for him to sleep in, and for one night his parents let him do just that. As he slept out under the stars, looking up at the twinkling lights through the branches overhead, he was sure that was how the early cave people must have felt.

David pulled his attention back to the classroom, checking the clock once more. He did so three more times before the bell rang loudly. The classroom rose frantically to their feet, all rushing in a stampede towards the door in opposition to the teacher's cries to slow down. It was Thursday and that meant his Scout meeting. He couldn't wait to tell his friends about his firearms badge. So, with all the energy of an unleashed ten-year-old, David charged through the hall, bag halfway zipped and a flurry of students blurring past.

Chapter 8

"...So I says to her, I didn't write the ticket, I just made what was on it. And it ain't my fault your customer doesn't know the difference between over-easy and over-hard..."

Cheryl looked across the dining room table to Mike, shaking her head empathetically. "Wow..."

David sat between them and was working the back end of a hot dog into his mouth. Another sat on the plate in front of him with a small pile of oven-warmed tater-tots resting against it.

"Well," Cheryl said. "Mavis says she caught the Miller boys smoking dope out back of the arcade a few days ago. Damn near had a conniption. Cops were called out and everything. The whole nine yards."

Mike swallowed the last bite of his hot dog, reaching down and taking a sip from his Pabst Blue Ribbon. "Well, I suppose my first question would be, what was old Mavis doing snooping around the back of a video arcade in the first place? Ain't nothin' there for anybody over sixteen anyhow."

"Oh, who knows," Cheryl replied with a smirk, shaking her head lightly. "You know Mavis, though. That nose is always gotta be somewhere it don't belong."

"What's *dope*?"

Mike shot a quick glance to his wife before turning his gaze to David. "Oh," he answered, the smile on his face spreading. "I think your mother might know a little more about that than I do."

Below the table, Cheryl's foot swung out, connecting solidly with her husband's shin. Mike winced, looking back to her and mouthing, *ow!*

"It's another word for marijuana," Cheryl answered.

David looked at her for a moment before replying with an unenthusiastic, "Oh." Then he turned his attention to the second hot dog.

"So," Mike asked, smiling at David. "Are you excited about tomorrow?"

David glanced between the two of them, the hot dog poised and ready just two inches from his mouth. "Yep." Then he leaned forward, taking a massive bite.

"Good," Mike said, turning his eyes back to his wife. "Then I think maybe you should finish up your dinner and get to bed a little early so you have your energy for tomorrow." Mike finished the sentence with a wink to Cheryl that went unnoticed by their son. A thin flush appeared on his wife's cheeks.

"Okay," David said, taking another bite.

"You still plannin' on pickin' up that extra shift next week?" Cheryl asked, taking a sip from her cup and setting it back down.

"I was thinkin' about it," Mike replied. "With Christmas just a few weeks away. Figured it couldn't hurt."

"You know we're not doing that bad, right?"

Mike knew. They'd both been making okay, Cheryl a bit more. They'd managed to put a few grand away in savings over the last year and if she got the raise she had been waiting for, they'd be able to stash even more away. Cheryl wanted a cabin, something small and tucked away, a place they could disappear to once or twice a year for a few days or a week. They'd stayed at one a few years back, up on the mountain. Ever since then Cheryl had been pinching pennies here and there, tucking away what she could. Prices weren't that bad, and though Mike had suggested them selling the trailer and getting an actual house, she had argued that they were already here, that the trailer was paid off and they only had a couple hundred a month for lot space, and that a cabin would be far more enjoyable in the long run. *'Imagine having our* own *place to go in the summer. Not having to worry about finding a campsite, or driving around all night because the campgrounds are full. Not having to sleep in a tent...'* Mike didn't see the allure, but he could see the joy in her face when she spoke about it, talking about how she would furnish it, and how they could sit around and play Monopoly or Parcheesi next to the fireplace. The way her face lit up at the mere mention was enough for him to agree.

"I know," Mike replied. "Just figured it'd be a little more for us to put away."

Cheryl smiled.

David shoved the last of his hot dog into his mouth, chewing quickly. "Is it okay if I play my game for a little while?" He punctuated his sentence with a small belch.

"Piggy!" his mom exclaimed, her face scrunching.

"Sorry mom."

"I suppose," Mike replied. "But don't stay up too late. We're up at the crack of dawn and I don't wanna hear you complaining about how you're *tired* the whole way there."

"Okay," David replied, sliding his chair out.

"You're not gonna eat those?" Mike asked, glancing down at the small pile of tater tots still sitting on the plate.

"No. I'm full."

"Alright," he smirked, waving his fingers towards him. "Give 'em here. I'll finish 'em"

"Okay." David held his plate out so his dad could sweep the tots off with his fork.

"Leave the plate in the sink, I'll take care of the dishes."

"Thanks, Dad," David replied, making his way to the sink and setting his plate in. He ran a small amount of water on top and turned, quickly making his way towards his room.

"Hey," Mike called out as David strode past.

David stopped, turning back.

"Aren't you forgetting something?"

"Oh," David said, mindfully. "Sorry."

He stepped back, leaned out and gave his mom a quick peck on the cheek. "Night Mom."

"Good night sweetheart," Cheryl returned.

David turned again and rushed off to his room. A moment later the door shut and the dining room fell quiet.

"He's a good kid, ain't he?" Cheryl asked, staring into the empty hallway before facing Mike once more. Mike smiled.

"Comes from good stock."

Cheryl's own warm smile grew.

"Whatta ya say we go get some more practice in?"

"Oh really," Cheryl replied, a small bite to her lower lip telling Mike everything he needed to hear.

"I think I'll take care of the dishes in the morning."

"No," Cheryl countered playfully. "You can wash the dishes. I need to go get ready."

"Yes ma'am!" Mike downed the last of his beer and stood. "Take your plate?"

"Yeah." Cheryl lifted her plate up. "I'm done."

Mike took the remaining tater tot and tossed it into his mouth before stacking her plate onto his and making his way to the sink.

A moment later Cheryl's hand edged around him, setting her glass in the sink before lowering down and gently grazing across the zipper of his pants. Mike groaned softly.

"Don't take too long with those," Cheryl advised, pulling her hand away and heading back towards their bedroom.

Chapter 9

Later that night, Mike and Cheryl were lying in bed. The small lamp on the nightstand cast a warm glow throughout the room, and from the hallway came the familiar *whoosh* of the wall furnace kicking on. Mike was reading through one of his Executioner series books. An ex-military special forces soldier named Mack Bolan was waging a one-man-war on the mafia and killing his way to the top. Beside him, Cheryl flipped through the latest issue of Country Living, her trial subscription awarded by the Publisher's Clearing House giving her a bountiful number of ideas for their soon-to-be new cabin.

Mike lowered his book, dog-earing a corner and closing it. He let his arm drop down, the book landing in his lap as he stared at the ceiling for a moment. Then he took one deep breath, exhaling sharply and turned his face to his wife. "I kind of told David I'd teach him to shoot today…"

He braced himself.

In an instant Cheryl's gaze was upon him, the magazine landing on her lap with a soft slap. "You're serious? Mike, we talked about this."

Mike was grateful that David was asleep. It meant that the conversation had to remain civil. It wasn't that either of them ever yelled or raised their voices against one another, but certain times their arguments could get heated.

"He's not a little boy anymore sweetheart. I mean, look at him. He is very quickly becoming a little man." He paused, sighing. "Your dad taught you how to shoot when you were eight…"

"Yeah," Cheryl replied, her eyebrows lifting. "And that same man used to shoot at people with a shotgun who would sneak in and try to steal watermelons from our patch."

"I just think it might be time to let him grow up a little." He paused then, a slight hesitation that ultimately didn't keep him from voicing a bit of his and David's earlier conversation. "And, I think it'd be good for him to have something to rub into that Jenkins kid's face."

"Really...?" Cheryl asked, her brow furrowing tightly. "Is that what this is about? Our boy one upping the *famous* Tommy Jenkins?" She quieted for a breath, then repeated, "Really?"

"Oh hell," Mike replied with a drawn smirk. "Everybody knows that kid's a spoiled brat. Ever since his mamma divorced that rich lawyer and took all his money, he's been parading that around town, bragging and rubbing it into all the other kid's faces. It'd be good to have somebody rub his face in something for once." He shook his head lightly, a small grin spreading across. "Why not let David be the one to do it?"

Cheryl sighed heavily. "I just worry about him. He's growing up so quick. In no time he's gonna be sneaking out at night, going to parties. Running around with girls..." She paused in thought. "I just. I want a little more time to remember him as the sweet, innocent little boy before he becomes..."

"Becomes what?"

"You know. A raging teenager full of testosterone and hormones."

"Oh, I know," Mike said mockingly. "Lord help us as he grows up like a normal kid."

Cheryl reached out and slapped her hand lightly against Mike's chest. "You know what I mean. Don't be a dick."

Mike smiled, his expression softening. "I know. I'm gonna miss it too." He reached out, taking her hand in his and squeezing softly. "And just so you know, I told him that he had to keep his grades at a B or above for the rest of the year, or it wouldn't happen."

Cheryl stared at him, her gaze working back and forth between his eyes. "And he agreed to that?"

"Of course he did," Mike assured her. "Fist bump and everything."

She let out a heavy sigh, her gaze wavering to the bed for a moment. "Okay."

"Come here," Mike said, pulling her close.

Cheryl scooted closer, resting her head on his chest as he began to run his fingers through her hair.

"He really is the best thing that's happened to us, huh?"

Mike nodded softly. "Yeah. Yeah, he is."

"I'm just scared, that's all."

"I know sweetheart," Mike acknowledged. "It's gonna be a blink of an eye before he's only coming home once a year to visit, or calling on the phone to say hi. That's why we have to enjoy this as much as we can while we have it."

Cheryl ran her fingers lightly across his chest, making small circles. "You're sure we're doing good?"

"As parents?"

"Yeah."

Mike scoffed with a smile. "Think about ours…"

"I know," she murmured, her fingers halting. "I just worry."

"I know babe," he replied. "I think we're doing great." He adjusted his gaze to meet hers. "You're an amazing mom, Cheryl. Way better than yours ever was. He's a lucky boy."

She nodded, resting her face back on his chest. "Thanks."

"Oh sweetheart," he said softly, pulling her tightly in. "You are beautiful and kind. David and I are the luckiest men in the world."

Cheryl smiled, listening as her husband's heart beat softly in his chest. He was right. Her mother hadn't been the picture of a perfect parent. She was quick to raise a hand and had left welts across her backside on more than one occasion. Her mother was a drinker and quick tempered, a bad combination. Her father had been present, but absent. Her home growing up was a well-defined matriarchy ruled with a swift hand and harsh judgment. She promised herself almost every day that she would do better, and it felt like the weight of the world was lifted off her chest every time Mike reassured her that she was. She knew she may not be the best mother in the world, but she would be damn-far better than hers was.

"I know I should have run it by you first. Sorry."

Cheryl let go of a weighted exhale once more, the irritation releasing across Mike's chest. "It's okay. I trust you and your judgment. If you think he's ready, then he's ready."

Mike nodded. He reached out and clicked his lamp off. The pair lay there for the next few minutes, enjoying each other's soft caresses as sleep playfully tugged at the back of their eyes. When the gentle twitches from his wife's legs told him she had fallen asleep, he carefully pulled his arm from beneath her neck, rolled over and fell asleep himself.

Chapter 10

The sun rose on what may have been one of Mike's favorite days of the year. The early light of dawn was just filtering through the kitchen window as he prepared their lunches of ham and cheese sandwiches, bananas, and soda. He'd woken up early, a half hour before his alarm went off like he did every morning on Tree Day. Clockwork. And just like he did every time, as was tradition, he had turned the alarm off and allowed his wife to get a little more sleep. David however had woken up at seven on the dot and was making his way sleepily into the living room, his G.I. Joe pajamas still bunched up around his calves.

"Hey kiddo," Mike greeted, glancing across the kitchen.

"Morning Dad," David yawned, rubbing the sleep from his eyes.

"You excited about today?"

"Mhm," David mumbled as he stepped into the kitchen. Mike placed the last sandwich in a small plastic sandwich bag and set it on top of the other two.

"Did you get enough sleep?"

David nodded. "Yeah." He then opened the fridge door and pulled out the carton of orange juice, twisting the cap off and taking two large gulps.

"Don't let your mother catch you drinking out of the carton like that. You know she hates that."

David took one last quick swig before capping the carton and putting it back in the fridge.

"Breakfast is ready," Mike announced, glancing at the towel covered plate warmly hiding a large stack of pancakes beneath. There was a pan on the stove that held the six scrambled cheesy eggs, with another pan flipped upside down on top to keep them from going cold too quickly.

"Thanks Dad," David replied, making his way to the table.

David pulled the chair out slowly, the legs squeaking across the linoleum. Then he climbed atop and slid it in. He'd stayed up later than he'd wanted to, but he had to finish that last level. His parents had gotten him the new video game system for his birthday earlier that year. He remembered pulling the wrapping paper off and seeing just the single word on the box, black metal on silver. Nintendo. That had been the first night he'd ever stayed awake until the sun came up. Thankfully it had been summer vacation, so his parents had allowed it just that once. He'd spent the entire night drinking soda and chomping everything that had come into Yoshi's path, the small green dinosaur ridden by the game's plumber protagonist. It had been one of the greatest nights of his life. Now, he was allowed to play after his homework was finished and had to be done by eight for bedtime. He still only had two games. His parents said they were expensive and they were saving up for something big. Still, they let him rent one every few weeks when they went to Blockbuster that he could keep for an entire week.

David's thoughts were pushed away by a plate being set down in front of him.

"How's your game?" his dad asked, setting a fork down beside the plate.

"It's good," David answered, diving into his breakfast.

"Is your mom up yet?"

"I don't know," David shrugged, his reply something more of a connected set of sounds for Mike to figure out than actual words.

"Well," Mike continued, making his way back to the stove to prepare his plate. "You got everything you're gonna wear?"

"Mhm," David grunted through a mouthful of pancakes.

"It's gonna be cold. Got a foot of snow a few days ago up there."

David set the fork down, taking a sip from the glass of milk his dad had set down. "I know Dad. It always is. I've got my thick jacket, my beanie, gloves, thick socks and an extra sweater just in case."

"Atta boy," Mike smiled, scooping a spoonful of eggs onto his plate. A moment later Cheryl came walking into the dining room, her robe pulled tightly to her form.

"Morning sweetheart," Mike said, his eyes working over the curves of her nightgown.

"Morning hon," she responded. "And how did *you* sleep?" she asked, moving to rustle David's hair with her fingers. David flinched back, giving her a smirk.

"Oh, I'm sorry," she intoned, glancing at Mike who shook his head with a grin. She pulled her chair out and took her seat.

"Coffee?" Mike asked.

Cheryl nodded.

A short time later the family had finished up breakfast. Cheryl and David went to get ready while Mike cleaned up in the kitchen. He had already cleared space for the tree earlier that morning. The green metal stand was in place and waiting for the tree to go atop. Mike finished up the dishes, drying and putting them away when David stepped back into the living room, jacket zipped up tight and beanie puled snugly down over his ears.

"I'm ready," he declared, moving to take a seat on the couch.

A minute later Cheryl emerged from the hallway. She was bundled up, her puffy white and blue jacket zipped all the way up to the chin, her knit beanie pulled down to her collar in the back, and a thick scarf wrapped around her neck holding it all in place. She was wearing her puffy snow pants and had the legs tucked into her furry snow boots.

Mike stifled a small chuckle.

"What, Mike?"

"Well," he replied, smiling at David. "It looks like your mother is all prepared for our trip to the Antarctic."

"Oh, shut up," Cheryl shot back with a smirk.

"Hey David," Mike said, placing the last of the plates in the cupboard. "Would you mind starting to put some of this stuff in the car for me? I need to have a quick chat with your mom."

"Yeah, Dad." David rose to his feet and made his way to the kitchen. He took the small lunch bag and walked to the door, grabbing the saw that was propped against it. He opened the door, a cold blast of air forcing its way past, and stepped out.

"Everything okay?" Cheryl asked, concern moving to her tone.

Mike turned and smiled, wiping his hands on his pants. "I just wanted to say thank you. I really do appreciate you letting me drag you guys out in the woods every year like this. It means... It means a lot to me. My parents used to do it with me, and it makes me happy to be able to keep that tradition going with my family."

Cheryl smiled, walking towards her husband. "I know Mike," she said, stopping close. "You know I just tease you right? I don't really have a problem with it."

"I know." Mike put his hands on her shoulders. "I just wanted to say thank you. That's all."

"That's sweet. Thank you, Mike," Cheryl smiled. "Though it would be a lot easier just to go to Chambers like everyone else..."

"Oh, be quiet," Mike smiled.

Cheryl grinned, leaning in to kiss him. They stood there, their lips pressed warmly against each other as they held each other tightly.

"I love you, Mike," Cheryl said as she pulled back. "And I'm pretty sure that of all the crazy fetishes a husband could have, I'm really lucky it's just this."

"Oh, you just wait," Mike teased. "We still have a lot of years to figure out what those are."

Cheryl smiled and pushed him against his shoulder. "Oh, be quiet."

Mike grinned.

"Let's not push it."

The smile on Mike's face grew. "So, what do you say we go get ourselves a tree?"

"Yay," Cheryl cheered blandly with mock enthusiasm.

David was just loading the last of their things in the back of the station wagon; a gallon jug of water and the spool of twine, when his parents made their way of their house and locked the door.

"We ready?" Mike called out as he stepped towards the car. "We got everything we need?"

"I think so," David nodded, reviewing his mental checklist. *Saw, twine, lunch, folding pocket knife, water.*

"Saw's in there?"

"Yeah dad. We have everything."

"That's my boy."

"Oh, he's *your* boy now?" Cheryl teased.

"When he's not getting into trouble."

David looked between them, unenthused.

"Well," Cheryl continued. "It's not getting any warmer out."

"No," Mike agreed. "That, it's not." He turned to David. "You ready?"

David smiled, nodding with enthusiasm.

"Then whatta ya say, we get this show on the road!"

David's smile grew and he charged around the side of the car, pulling the back door open and jumping in. He clicked his seatbelt and looked past his parents to the snow-covered yard. He didn't mind going out into the woods to get their tree. It made his parents happy, and that made him happy. He knew it was something important to them, and that one day, he may have a family of his own. He liked to think he would keep that tradition.

"OH! I almost forgot!" Mike exclaimed, startling both Cheryl and David. He reached up, pulling the rearview down to angle it back to David. "You got your scout book? I don't wanna forget to sign off on your backpacking and nature badges. We don't want old Tommy Jenkins getting *too* far ahead."

Cheryl shot him a look that he met with a silent grin.

"Got it right here," David confirmed, holding up the small backpack that was beside him.

Okay," Mike replied, "Whew."

David smiled, setting the bag back down as his dad readjusted the rear view and put the car into reverse.

They made their way down the small lane that was lined with a dozen other mobile homes. Thankfully, the park manager had grated and salted the lanes earlier that morning. Moments later Mike was pulling the station wagon out onto the main road and the Connor family were making their way out of town.

Chapter 11

The air outside was crisp and sharp, the biting breath of winter pushed down the mountain in soft gusts of pristine air. Twenty minutes prior Mike had pulled off old highway fifty-six and they were making their way upwards, following the mild twists and turns that would eventually lead to the old logging road. Mike had come across it eight years prior. Cheryl cracked her window, just barely, and was feeling the crisp air chill her cheek.

"Mom," David called out from behind. "It's cold!"

Cheryl let the chill settle into her for a moment longer, the thin numbness moving from her cheek towards her eye. Then she reached out and rolled the window up. It hit her at that moment. *Mom*. The single word felt foreign to her. She knew that David had been struggling the past year in his desperate attempt to shed his youthful childhood, and part of that self-fulfilling prophecy was the transition from being Mommy to just Mom. There was just something cold about it, the loss of two letters taking all the warmth behind the word with it.

"You think that's bad," Mike said, glancing into the rear-view. "Just wait till we get there. It's supposed to be one of the coldest winters yet."

David scowled, lowering his gaze back to the book that bounced lightly in his hands.

"What you readin' back there?" Mike asked.

David stopped reading long enough to hold the book up so his dad could see the cover. "Wilderness survival," David replied.

"Oh yeah?" Mike said, watching as a step curve approached. "What's it got in it?"

David pulled his eyes away again. "Um. Like building fires, and snares and traps. How to fix yourself if you break your leg. It's cool."

"Well," Cheryl smiled. "I hope we won't be needing to use *that* book while we're up here."

"Me too," David replied.

"Aww," Mike pouted. "You don't think it'd be cool to be stuck out in the woods for a week or two?"

"No," David replied flatly.

"Oh, well I kind of always wanted to go out with nothing but a pack on and a knife. See how long I could survive on my own."

"I think this could be the perfect opportunity," Cheryl smiled. "You go ahead and go off into the woods, but leave me the keys. David and I will come check on you in a month. How's that sound?"

Mike smiled, maneuvering the wagon around a sharp turn. "Don't tempt me."

"Hey," Cheryl added. "Are you sure the car's gonna be able to make it up here this year? All joking aside. There's a lot more snow than usual. I really don't wanna get stuck out here."

"We're okay," Mike comforted. "We got chains on, a spare tire. Tank's full and the battery's only a couple years old. You ain't got nothing to worry about sweetheart." He paused. "Besides, we've got Kit Carson sitting in our back seat. I think we'll be just fine." Mike smiled, glancing in the mirror to David who didn't lift his gaze from the book.

Cheryl folded her arms across her chest with a huff. "If you say so. But if we get stuck, you're the one walking back to town while David and I stay in a warm car."

"Like it would have been any other way," Mike replied, looking out of his window.

A thin line of trees peeled back, exposing the snow-covered valley below. There was a small frozen reservoir in the distance, a silver sheen reflecting off the ice. Snow-topped trees spread out for as far as the eye could see, tiny ashen bristles rising up. Iron mountain wasn't particularly desolate or isolated, but it was a good half-hour outside of town. The road that led them to their tree spot was about an hour more at the speed they were traveling, just over fifteen miles an hour. They probably could have gone faster, but they were in no hurry, and the last thing Mike wanted was to come around a blind turn doing twenty and collide into a truck heading down. There were some areas where the road dropped off the side a hundred-feet to the bottom.

"I always hate this part," Cheryl said, looking past Mike to where only open sky and nothing beyond lay beyond his window.

"I got this," Mike replied.

David lifted his gaze, looking out of the window for a moment. The pure whiteness was mesmerizing. Above, the light blue had been replaced with a dull slate. Grey blended with snow-white to create a blurred palate of nothingness. It looked so calm and peaceful, but was also scary. He knew how cold it was out there. Your feet could freeze in no time and you could get hyp… hypa… *Hypathermal.* You'd freeze. That's why he was studying how to make fire. Bow drill, flint spark, hand-drill method. He'd read the section three times already, committing it to memory as best as he could. If they did get stuck out there, he could build a fire and keep them warm while his dad went for help.

The air chilled further the higher they got. At over five-thousand feet they were already surrounded by air in the low forties. Wind chill probably dropped it another five to ten degrees more. David shifted, pulling his jacket down a bit, pressing it tighter against him.

A short time later the car pulled off the two-lane road leading up onto a smaller one-lane. A plow had come through once at the beginning of the snow, but hadn't been back since. There were another two sets of tire tracks leading up and Mike maneuvered his car to match, hoping that the other tracks would help give him traction. The wagon had a wide stance and from what it looked, the other vehicles had been trucks, so the T&C fell right in.

"Are you sure about this?" Cheryl asked a minute later. "We've never been up here with snow like this."

"It'll be fine," Mike replied. "Like I said, we've got chains on and it's only about another half-mile. We'll be there before you know it."

"Okay…"

They traveled slowly down the single-lane road, the car bouncing along to the unseen bumps below. An endless field of white and brown surrounded them, splashes of dark green pine peeking through. The woods surrounding were quiet, solitary. They were Lewis and Clark, and this was their trail.

A few minutes later the road came to an end and a large, circular clearing fell into view. The other tracks followed the edge, circling back. It had been one truck, in and out.

Mike followed the tracks, turning the circle and stopping half way. Then he reached out, his hand hovering over the key for a moment before grasping it and killing the engine.

"And," he smiled. "We're here." He turned his face to Cheryl. "See? We didn't get stuck."

Cheryl stared back at him. "We haven't tried to leave yet, have we…?"

"Oh, you calm down," he smiled, reaching out to tap her on the leg. "Well," he said, craning his head back to David. "Let's go."

David stepped out of the car, his feet dropping into the calf-high snow. He immediately felt the cold winter air bite into him. The soft wind was sharp, like thin razors drawn against the skin. His breath hovered out in front of him and for a moment he stood, exhaling clouds and pretending he was a great dragon preparing to breath a plume of fire.

"It's chilly, huh?" Mike said, stepping around towards the back of the car.

"It's not so bad," David replied, sending one last breath clouding out.

"Speak for yourself," his mom said, stepping out of the car. "I'm freezing my butt off."

"Well," Mike replied, opening the rear hatch outward. "We're only gonna be out here for an hour or so. I think you'll survive."

"Hmph," she snorted, her breath shooting downwards from her nostrils.

"Here," Mike said, reaching into the back. "You wanna take this?" He pulled the small spool of twine out and tossed it to David, who caught it clumsily. "You got your knife, right?"

David reached down and tapped his jacket pocket. He felt the small wood and steel object folded inside. He nodded firmly.

"It is a cold one this year," Cheryl said, stopping a few feet away to admire the silent wilderness that surrounded them.

"Record breaking the guy on the news was saying," Mike added, pulling the saw out. "We good to go?"

David nodded, moving one hand to his backpack.

"Then whatta ya say we go find our tree?"

David smiled, moving to a jog through the snow and kicking up a flair of rooster-tails as he charged forward towards the trees.

"It looks like our scout's gonna lead the way," Mike said, looking to Cheryl with a smile, who returned it warmly.

David charged through the snow, passing the first cluster of trees before slowing. He could feel the air icing his lungs with each breath and a thin sweat had already broken out beneath his sweater. He slowed his pace, allowing his feet to trudge through the snow. The woods around them were quiet, silent almost, if it weren't for the sound of the air breathing through the trees. The ground sparkled, an endless field of crushed diamonds shimmering under the dull light that filtered down through the clouds above. David kicked out, his boot exploding through a small drift and sending a plume of frosty snow outwards. He watched as the icy trails lifted out and then fell to the snow below. He didn't mind the cold. He loved sledding and tubing, building snowmen and having snowball fights. He didn't mind bundling up or getting wet. A lot of the other kids hated it. They'd stay inside all day and complain about how cold it was. But not him. He liked to pretend that he was on an arctic adventure, the first person to ever travel the frozen tundra. The snow made it feel like that. There were no footprints, no trails, just an endless plane of white spread between the trees. He was at that moment, the first person to break through.

"How far are we going?" Cheryl asked Mike who was about fifty feet behind David.

"I figure not too far," Mike answered, calling ahead to David. "Stay where we can see you!"

"I know Dad," David yelled back without slowing his pace.

"Don't worry, we'll be drinking hot chocolates and decorating the tree before you know it."

"Better," Cheryl replied. "You can sneak some of that brandy we got stashed away into mine."

Mike smiled, following his son's footprints. "That's not a bad idea. Not a bad idea at all."

Up ahead the trees pulled back into a small clearing. David slowed to a stop, taking in the open space in wonder. A moment later his parents walked up, stopping beside him.

"You know," David said, his eyes sparkling. "I bet Tommy Jenkins never gets to do this."

Cheryl looked at Mike who smiled, reaching out and putting his hand on David's shoulder. "No. From what you said, they get their tree from Chambers." He paused, a grin spreading across his face. "I wonder if he gets a badge for that, too?"

David laughed, the sound filling the clearing and echoing off the trees. "That's funny Dad!"

Cheryl smiled, squeezing Mike's arm.

"Hey Dad," David said, his hand raising up in a snap with one finger extended. "Look!"

David traced the boy's line to a tree just at the opposite edge of the clearing. Standing just taller than him like the perfect image of Christmas, conical to a sharp tip, was a beautiful fir tree.

Mike didn't even have time to respond before David was blasting across the clearing, closing in on the tree.

"Well," Mike said with a light smirk. "Looks like we found our tree."

"It's perfect," Cheryl replied softly, watching as David plowed through the snow.

Mike smiled, reaching down to slap his wife's butt lightly. "Come on," he said, jumping forward before she could slap him playfully in the chest. "Don't just stand there, we got a tree to cut."

Cheryl watched as Mike took off after David. She felt a loving warmth course through her. Those were her men, and she loved them both fiercely.

"So whatta ya think kiddo?" Mike asked as he approached where David was standing. "Is this the one?"

David eyed the tree, nodding. "Yeah. This is the tree."

"Well," Mike replied, holding the saw out. "You ready to earn those presents?"

"Yes sir," David replied, taking the saw.

Cheryl walked up, giving Mike *the look*. The year prior he had decided that David was old enough to cut down the tree himself. He and Cheryl had come to a slight disagreement over the thought and it had led to Mike cutting the tree, but letting David give it the final push over. This year though...

"It's fine," Mike said in that tone that always seemed to work somehow.

"First you tell him you're gonna teach him to shoot," Cheryl whispered, leaning slightly closer. "Now you're gonna let him cut his fingers off. What next? You want enroll him in the military?"

"Oh, come on," Mike said, squinting at her.

"It's just...a lot. At once."

"I know sweetheart, but we have to let him grow up sometime."

David was oblivious to the conversation his parents held. He was focused, his saw already moving back and forth in a flurry of movement as he made the perfect cut. He'd scooped the snow around the base aside so he could get as close to the ground as possible, just like his dad had shown him. Again and again, he sawed back and forth. His arms were tired and his back was now wet with sweat. But he didn't stop. He just kept sawing, over and over, until he heard his dad call out, "That's good!" from behind.

David stopped, edging back and standing up.

"You wanna give it the push?" Mike asked, looking at Cheryl.

"I didn't bring my gloves."

"You can use mine," he said, moving to remove them.

"No," she assured him, reaching out to stop his hand. "It's fine. You guys do it."

"Okay, but you're missing out on the best part."

She smiled. "I don't wanna be washing pine sap off my hands for the next three days. I just had my nails done."

"It's a fir," Mike corrected, "but it's okay. We get it."

She smirked at him, placing her hands back in her pockets.

"All right kiddo," Mike said, moving next to the tree and putting one hand at the top. "On three."

David set the saw down and put his hands on the base of the tree.

"One. Two. Three!"

The two of them pushed together, sending the tree *cracking* to the side as the thin remainder of the trunk broke free.

"Timber!" Mike yelled, his voice echoing out loudly.

David chuckled.

"Alright," Mike said. "Now the not-so fun part. You got that twine?"

David reached into his bag, pulling the twine out.

"Now I'll lift it up. You get it under there, then all we have to do is wrap it tightly and we're good to go."

"Okay," David smiled, grabbing the end of the twine and unrolling a small length.

"Just like a carpet," Mike said. "Roll and wrap."

Cheryl stood there, watching in loving admiration as the two most amazing men in her life wrapped up the tree and tied it securely.

"Now let's get this back to the car," Mike said, glancing at his wife. "Here's how I earn *my* presents." The insinuation in his words flew unnoticed by David, but renewed the flush in his wife's cheeks.

Mike reached down and hoisted the tree up, dropping it onto his shoulder. "Now, mush!" he barked, starting forward.

Chapter 12

The Town & Country sat lonely in the clearing, the lack of snow atop making it look odd and out of place with the rest of the snow-covered surroundings. The hollow stillness in the air was shattered by the sound of laughter approaching.

"I'm not sure I can make it!" Boomed the words from the trees. "I just don't have the power!"

David laughed, amused by his father's grave slaughter of the Scottish accent. A moment later the family emerged from the trees, smiles carried between them. Mike dropped the tree down from his shoulder to rest it against the car. All he needed to do was lift it on top, run the twine through the windows and they'd be home in time for lunch. This was going to be a good year. He hadn't told David yet, but they'd gotten him the BMX bike he'd had his eye on for the last six months. Every time they went past the bike section David would be sure to point it out, telling them how cool it was, and that this friend and that one just got a bike, asking when he was going to get his own. Little did he know, the last three months they'd been paying off the layaway. One last payment and it would be wrapped up and below... Well, behind the tree. They'd gotten him a new video game as well, but they knew the excitement of that, as well as his time to play it, would quickly change the moment he opened the large gift. Santa of course, had gotten him a couple of smaller gifts. While David asserted a disbelief in the existence of the phantom chimney stalker, they could tell he was still on the fence about it. He had friends who'd been telling him the truth, but Mike kind of felt David holding onto hope just for the feeling of mystique it gave him.

"Just gotta get this hoisted up, and we're as good as drinking hot chocolates."

"Dad..."

David stood nearby. He'd tossed his backpack into the back seat and knelt down to ball up some snow he was going to send flying deep into the woods. That's when movement caught his eye and he turned to see another man walking down the road in their direction. Something about the man made him feel funny, a sour knot tightening in his stomach. The man was wearing a jean jacket with dirty white fur on the collar and blue jeans. He had long wavy hair that mussed up at his shoulders and his gaze was locked, moving between them. There was no smile, no friendliness and he was walking quickly, following one of the tire tracks. "Dad," David repeated, warning his dad who was focused on getting the tree on top of the car. The snowball dropped to the ground at his side.

Mike hoisted the tree, shifting it to the middle of the roof and looked over to David. There was something in his tone that concerned him.

"Dad," David said again. "Someone's coming."

Mike traced his son's finger to the man approaching them. He was only about twenty yards away.

The man raised his hands in the air as he neared them, an odd smile flashing across his face. "Sorry folks," he called out, still approaching. "Didn't mean to sneak up on ya'll like that."

Mike lowered his hands, wiping the snow and sap on his pant legs.

"Just that, well, my truck don't wanna start. Think it's on account of the cold. Old battery, you know."

Cheryl shifted closer to Mike.

"I was wondering if I might be able to hitch a ride with ya'll back to town?"

Mike watched, noticing that the man's gaze kept working between him and Cheryl, lingering longer on her than himself. There was something behind his eyes that didn't sit well with him; maybe his tone, maybe just intuition. Mike could see that the man wasn't showing any sign of slowing down and he stole a glance at the large hunting knife hanging on his belt. The air around them grew colder.

Cheryl reached up, placing her hand on his shoulder and squeezed, a silent gesture shared between them for him to be careful, that he wasn't the only one that was having a bad feeling.

"What brings you up here?" Mike asked, standing his ground as the man drew closer. "Huntin' season ain't for about another few weeks."

The man finally stopped about ten feet away. "Ah," he said, briefly eying Cheryl again. "You know. I like to get away every now and again." His gaze now slithered over her as he spoke. "Can't argue with the privacy these woods offer. I kinda like it."

The grip on Mike's shoulder stiffened.

"I guess I just didn't think to check my battery before I left. You know how these old cars can be."

David stood behind the car, where he had been when he'd seen the man first approaching. A strange nervousness held him tight. Worry? Fear? He listened to the way the man spoke and heard the tone in his father's voice as he responded. His dad was worried. He hadn't heard that tone many times, but he knew it enough to tell they were in trouble.

"If you don't mind me asking," Mike said, his gaze not leaving the man. "How's it you ended up down this road?" He shrugged, glancing around. "Not exactly the direction I'd have thought to go lookin' for help."

The man stared back, a nearly imperceptible squint flashing through his eyes. "Well," he said, his voice shifting slightly. "I's camped a short ways from here. Heard your car." Again, the man's eyes moved to Cheryl, sliding down her partially concealed figure before lifting back to Mike. "Nice boy you got back there," the man continued, the words almost snapping out. "How old is he? Ten, eleven?"

Mike stared back. He'd been fine with the man approaching, even tolerable of the looks he was throwing his wife, but bringing his boy into it… "Where'd you say you were camped again?"

The man pulled his eyes from David and snapped them back to Mike. Another squint flashed past, this one deep and visible. "I didn't," he replied, pausing for a moment as he held Mike's gaze. "Look mister," the man said, his tone low, eyes unblinking. "Like I said, I ain't lookin' for no trouble. But it'd be mighty advantageous if I could get that ride."

Cheryl squeezed again and Mike lowered his hand, pushing her slightly behind him. "I apologize. I'd love to offer you that ride, but unfortunately the car's already pretty full. Once we get that tree inside, 'fraid there won't be any room left." Mike paused, feeling the panic coming from his wife. "But tell you what. We're headed straight back to town, and the moment we get back, I'll go on and send the sheriff out this way to give you a hand. Won't be no problem at all."

The man's hand moved to the handle of his knife and Mike felt the ice begin to flow through his veins.

"Well," the man started, his knuckles tightening around the handle. "Actually…" His face winced, his teeth clenching for a moment as a look of eating something sour flashed past. "See, that is gonna be a problem. Me and sheriffs, we don't get along none too well." He paused, his gaze sliding to Cheryl, staying locked on her form as his eyes slowly moved down to her chest. "And a pretty little thing like you got there… I'd be real sad to see her leave without getting to know her a bit first." He regarded Mike again. "It does get *mighty* lonely out here."

Frozen realization struck Mike and he started forward, Cheryl's hand desperately trying to pull him back.

"Mike, don't," she whimpered.

Mike glanced back at her, then turned his attention back to the man.

"I don't like the direction this conversation is heading," Mike said, his gaze narrowed. "Now why don't you go ahead and go on back the way you came. Ain't no need for this to get any worse."

"I think maybe you oughta listen to your little lady there," the man said, anger flashing. "I'm not taking too kindly to your tone either."

Mike grit his teeth. "Just leave us alone and go back to wherever you came from."

The man sneered, an audible growl coming from him. "No. I don't think I'm gon' do that."

In a flash, the man pulled the knife from his belt and jumped forward. Mike stepped to meet him, his hands moving up as a loud scream erupted from Cheryl. The man's hand shot out, blade first. Mike managed to get his hand around the man's wrist, shooting the other one out in an attempt to wrestle the blade free. Behind him he could hear his wife continue to scream. He struggled, the man's wrist as tightly as he could.

The man fought against the father trying to wrestle the blade from him. It wasn't the first time some bastard had tried that. All he needed to do was—

Mike screamed as the man's foot smashed against his knee, buckling his leg sideways and sending him dropping to the ground. The pain was intense and he had lost hold of the man's arm. He turned, fighting against the blinding pain in his leg to rise. But as soon as he turned his head he saw the blade swinging in a wide arc and felt the cold steel cut from one side of his neck to the other.

Cheryl's scream erupted to new heights, time flinching to a stop as she watched the blade slice through her husband's neck, the blood exploding outward. She watched as the man she loved brought his hands to his neck and listened to the gurgled gasps bubbling out as he struggled to pull air through his severed windpipe. Blood painted the snow below him red, steam rising up from the freshly spilled warmth. The screams wouldn't stop.

Behind the car, David watched in horror as the man cut his father's throat. He heard sounds he'd never heard before and stared as his dad tried desperately to seal the wound. Then he watched the other man step forward and plunge the knife deep into his daddy's chest. His mother screamed, a sound he'd never heard. Fear, panic, pain. David stood frozen, unable to move. Then the man started forward and the screaming stopped.

"David!" his mom screamed. "RUN!"

David stared as the man edged closer to his mom, the bloodied knife in his hand. Cheryl spun, taking one last glance at her husband who lay bleeding out on the ground. She charged to the front of the car, turning the corner and making it to the edge before a strong grip wrapped itself in her hair and pulled her back.

"DAVID, RUN!!!"

"Mom..." David whimpered, watching the man step backwards, dragging his mom by the hair as she kicked and struggled to get free.

"I love you David," Cheryl managed to cry, her eyes locked to her son standing frozen in the snow. "Now, *RUN!*"

David locked his gaze to the man, thinking of every horrible pain he could cause him, punching him in the face, kicking his crotch. Then he turned, tears streaming down his cold face in warm streams and he ran.

"That's right boy!" the man yelled. "Run!"

He turned his attention to the woman below. "Your mamma and I are gonna spend a little time together."

Chapter 13

Trees flashed past in a blur of greenish brown and white as David ran. The snow under his feet blasted out in shimmering plumes, exploding as his boots smashed through. He could hear his mother screaming behind him but he didn't stop. Something was inside him. It filled him, this feeling he'd never felt that was stronger than the worst nightmare and scarier that the scariest monster under his bed. The thing inside him screamed, begged and pleaded for him to run faster, to get away, to go as far as he could as fast as he could and to not ever look back. Even if he were able to take the fastest look to ever exist, pure panic and blinding fear drove him forward. The fear, and panic and heat tore at his chest, threatening to rip free as he ran.

All around him the forest pressed in, the trees taller than they had been and the forest denser. Branches reached out, slapping him hard across the face and every hidden root threatened to send him plummeting to the ground. But he pushed harder, his lungs ablaze, a salted fire in every breath he drew. David kept running until the screaming behind had either stopped, or was too far back to hear. Then he slowed to a stop, hunching forward as his hands caught his knees.

Deep shudders of warm air burst forth from his mouth, his breaths ragged and quick. His eyes were glued to the glittering snow beneath him and he could feel the heat from his body rising up. Steam came off of his face as the surrounding air bit at him sharply, the thick lines down his cheeks freezing cold. The only sounds he could hear were the air leaving his mouth in heavy pushes and his heartbeats pounding in his ear. He stayed there, hunched forward, for a moment. Then, he rose and spun, looking back in the direction he had come. He could see his footprints, a deep path leading off into the distance. His eyes worked desperately through the surrounding woods, taking in every direction at once. Only the silent forest peered back.

Off to his right in fifteen or so yards was a fallen tree, the trunk just large enough for him to hide behind. David moved his wobbly legs and raced towards it, climbing over and dropping down behind. He let his butt fall to the ground and leaned back against the cold wood, pressing his back against it. His gaze locked onto the snow a few feet away as his mind played and replayed the events that had just occurred. A welling of emotion overtook him as a thin chill worked through his jacket.

David sat there, sobbing loudly as the realization that his father had just been killed and bad things were happening to his mommy. Everything was wrong. Why? Why did that man do that? His daddy hadn't done anything to him. They didn't even know him. They'd never seen that man before. And why did he want to know his mom so badly? They weren't friends. It was obvious she didn't like him. Why would he force her like that? You can't do that. You don't. That's not how you treat someone you want to be friends with. That's what bullies do. He was a bully. No. Worse. He was a murderer.

* * *

"Now David, the Wild West wasn't only about gun-fights and Indians. It wasn't how it was in the movies," David's history teacher informed the prior year. "Well, not all. Some are pretty accurate. Do you think you can tell me what drove people like Billy the Kid and Boone Helm to do the things they did?"

David regarded the teacher as he considered his answer. "Because they wanted to be famous?"

Mr. Harper smiled back. "Well. Yes, David. I'm sure that had something to do with it. But there had to be something else that drove those men to do the things they did."

"Because they were crazy!"

Mr. Harper looked at the boy sitting behind David, shushing the laughter that had risen. "Yes Tommy," he replied. "That very well could have been part of the reason. But there had to have been something else."

"Because they wanted what other people had?" David answered sheepishly.

"Yes, David. That's called greed. And with greed comes envy. That is the most common thing that leads to murder. We can fantasize about those men all we want, create all these lavish stories and movies about them, but at the end of the day that's what they were; murderers."

"So, a murderer is someone that kills another person because they want what they have?"

"Not necessarily," Mr. Harper replied. "There are many reasons that drive people to murder someone. Sometimes they're not all that complicated at all. Sometimes people are just born that way. Ted Bundy, Jeffrey Dahmer. Those men didn't do the things they did because they wanted something from the people they killed. Well. Not techinically, but we're not going to get into that today. I'll save that for your high school teachers. No. They weren't taught to do those things, they just did. Some would argue they were just *born* that way."

"What happed to them?" David asked, possibly more intrigued than he should have been.

"Well. The same thing that should happen to every murderer. They were killed."

"So. If someone *murders* someone else. You should murder them?"

"It's not as simple as that David. They need to be proven guilty, go through a court trial. Then the judge can sentence their punishment. And yes, sometimes that is death if the crime is bad enough."

* * *

David sat there, the frozen ground pressing up through his pants into his bottom. His teacher's words worked their way through his head. That man was bad. He was like Ted Bundy and Billy the Kid. He was a murderer. He had murdered his daddy. He didn't want anything. They didn't have anything to take, 'cept for their tree, but there were a zillion trees he could have. He killed his daddy, and so he deserved to die.

The tears finally slowed as he thought about his mom and dad. They'd been so happy coming up, so excited to get their tree and to have their hot chocolates. Everything had been so perfect. And then that man had walked up. In an instant everything had gone bad. The thing that hurt David the most, was that there was nothing he could do. His father was strong, he'd seen him lift up the entire couch one time, and David could barely get one side to budge. If the other man was strong enough to kill his dad, then there was no way he was going to be able to beat him. His thoughts moved to his mother, and once again the tears began to flow.

Chapter 14

The sky overhead remained a dull slate, a swirling palate of grays with a hint of white just behind. The tips of the pines stretched upwards, just the very tops flaring green from the wind blowing the snow free. The air was quiet, cold and still. Below, a single tree lay wrapped in twine atop an old station wagon. Then a deep breathing broke the serene calm.

Just off to the side of the car the killer stood, his breaths heavy, bursts of steam coming from his lips. There was an uneasy calm on his face and his hands hung by his sides, blood dripping from the blade of the knife he held. He stood there for a moment before tilting his head back and exhaling thickly. Then he flicked his wrist, sending the knife stabbing into the snow below.

The man moved his hands to his waist, bringing the buttons on his jeans together and fastening them. He worked his belt shut as he let his gaze move down to the naked body of the woman below. Her brown hair was streaked red, and the pinkness of her exposed flesh contrasted brightly against the white beneath. The woman's pants were bunched loosely around her ankles, one leg pulled clear free. Her jacket had been ripped open and her shirt cut free. Her breasts were exposed and there were a series of deep, visceral puncture wounds between them where the man had plunged the knife a half-dozen times when he was finished. Open eyes stared tear-streaked into the trees off to the side.

The killer turned his head, looking past the car to where the small set of footprints led into the woods. Slowly, a small grin splayed his lips as his neck craned to the side, cracking softly. Cold eyes locked onto the dead woman, his smile not fading. "Well, sweetheart, guess we better wrap things up. Don't worry about your boy. I'll take care of him."

The man spun around, the smile fading from his face as his gaze followed the set of tracks leading into the woods. With a single breath, he started forward.

Chapter 15

David was still crouched behind the tree when he heard the first shouts. He didn't know how long he'd been there, but his bum was numb. He'd caught his breath some time before and his legs no longer felt like jelly.

"I like how your mamma put up a fight!"

David's head whipped to the side so fast he thought it would crack. The words were distant and barely discernable, but close enough to hear.

"Girl had some spunk in her!"

David tensed, the panic rising to a crescendo.

"A little more now!"

David listened as the man laughed at some uninterpreted joke. The feeling he had prior returned, telling him to get up and run, to flee and escape. The man was coming, the killer, the *murderer*.

David felt his breaths shorten, his heart beginning to pound again. He had to do something. He had to run. He knew that man was going to do to him what he did to his daddy. With that thought, he brought himself quickly to his feet and charged further into the trees.

In the woods behind, the man stalked the trail. Cold eyes watched in mild fascination as the path he followed led towards the boy. He had no fascinations with catching the kid, other than he couldn't leave him alive. He'd seen his face and knew he was camped close. It wouldn't do to have the little shit go running to the cops. *Another loose-end to tie up*, he thought as he followed the boy's trail. He'd never killed a kid before and a loose smirk crossed his lips at the thought.

He walked the next few yards, chuckling again at his joke. He didn't fancy himself the comedic type, but he sure could pull out a funny every now and then.

Just ahead he saw where the trail led to a large log and the telltale marks the kid had left when clamoring over. He slowed his pace, a thin smile growing across his lips as he quietly pulled the knife from its scabbard. He edged forward, sneaking quietly. He enjoyed this game; it was one he was good at. The next few paces went slowly as he positioned himself at the end of the fallen tree. Then with a wide grin, he jumped around the edge of the tree and shouted, "Gotcha!"

The space where the boy should have been hiding was empty. His eyes locked to the trail of footprints leading further into the trees. He traced the path, letting his gaze move to the mountain rising up behind. The smile grew. "Go on boy!" he shouted, his words dropping to a whispered growl as the grin morphed into something else, something darker. "I got all the time in the world..."

David blasted out of the tree line. He needed to find high ground. Ten feet in front of him was a small river. Ice covered the top, working around the large rocks that jutted upwards. He could hear the water flowing beneath and imagined how cold it would be. His gaze worked frantically over the frozen water, moving right, then left. He needed to get across. If he could get across, he could make his way to the mountain. If he could do that, he could get to the top, and from there he could see which way town was. He might be able to escape.

The snow had melted away from the small stones lining the river's edge. He looked upstream, his eyes tracing the frozen path, and saw where a cluster of rocks were just close enough together that he could use them to get across. But he knew that the man behind him was easily following his trail. He needed to confuse him, to cut the trail off. He had led him right to the river, and if he thought about using the crossing, then he had to assume the man would, too.

David looked back into the woods. The man was close enough that he had heard his voice before, so he needed to move quickly. He had to get across the river and on the hill before the man found him. The man had killed his father easily, so David knew that he would be much faster than him as well. With that thought, he turned and darted towards the crossing, using the exposed stones to conceal his tracks. He charged up the riverbank, sprinting towards the rocks. It took him less than a minute to arrive and in a breath's time he was scrambling to the first stone.

The rocks leading across were spaced a few feet apart. They stood at jagged angles, like stone teeth jutting up in a crooked smile. David got his feet onto the first, his foot slipping slightly against the ice that covered the side the river flowed against. He found his balance, his arms held out to his sides. He calculated the distance to the next rock and made a careful jump.

His feet landed on the stone, this one flatter than the prior. There was a thin layer of ice, but he easily avoided it. As he stood there, he looked down through it to the flowing water beneath. It was dark and moving fast. He couldn't see the bottom. He knew that one slip could send him plunging through, and once he was beneath the ice the current would pull him under and he would drown. But there was something much worse than drowning in a frozen river behind him, and it was closing in quickly. So, with that last thought he strategized his next jump, leaping to the jagged stone. His first foot caught, but his second slipped on the ice and he dropped, barely catching himself on the edge of the stone as his foot dropped to the river's ice below. It cracked, but he managed to pull himself up. He repeated the process two more times, but on the last stone his foot slipped, sending it sliding to the ice beneath. There was a soft *crack* and he felt the ice beneath give out. In an instant he was standing up to his thighs in the frozen current. The shock was immediate and he felt the river's teeth lunge deeply into his legs as the coldness clamped down. He scrambled, his hands desperately seeking any hold as the current tugged at his legs. A moment later they found the back edge of a rock and he began to hoist himself up. He could feel the current's unrelenting grasp yanking at his freezing ankles as it rushed past. Panic surged through him as his legs from the top of the knees down had already gone numb. It felt like they were burning.

David pulled desperately against the rock as he struggled to get one of his legs out of the water. Once he'd lifted the second one out he used the stone as leverage to stand up. He stood there, the adrenaline coursing through him in a raw and terrifying power. For a moment, David looked back at the woods where he had emerged. He then faced forward and took his last leap to the shore.

He turned his gaze to the mountain. It rose up, towering above, and he could see where a sharp craggy ravine ran from the bottom almost three-quarters of the way up. If he stayed in the ravine and used it to go up, it would be almost impossible for the man chasing him to see him. With that final thought he moved his frozen legs as fast as he could and took the first squishing step towards the slope.

Chapter 16

It was a short time later that the man emerged from the trees, the trail he had been following ending at the rocky shore. He slowed to a stop, his gaze narrowing as it moved up and down the bank. He looked down for some indication of which way the boy had gone, but only wet stones glared back. A thin smile returned to his cheeks and he lifted his gaze, carefully scanning the mountain in front of him. He enjoyed the chase, the hunt.

"You think you can hide from me boy?" he shouted, an angry crack running through his words. "These is *my* woods!!"

The man eyed the mountain a moment longer before looking back to the river. He studied the tree line, checking for any signs of a trail, but found only untouched snow beneath. "You gon' leave a trail sooner or later," he whispered, his gaze moving back to the mountain. "And I'm gonna be right here to find it."

The man turned, starting downstream and away from the crossing and the little boy scrambling up the mountainside.

David worked his way up the slope. It was steep and the silt and limestone beneath his feet slid out with every step. More than a few times he'd had to grasp the ravine slope to keep from sliding back down. Thin cuts dug into his hands and his legs were still numb, making the going even harder. Still, he forced himself, struggling to keep his upward momentum.

He made it up another fifteen feet when the rocks beneath his feet gave way. David went sliding backwards at least five feet before catching his grip. He lay there, stomach pressed against the cold mountainside. He was tired, out of breath and beyond cold. His legs had begun to tremble and he felt like someone was holding a torch to his feet. He'd never felt that kind of cold before. Sure, he'd jumped in a cold lake and had been left shivering by a fire for a few hours, but this the kind of cold where you couldn't feel the shoes around your feet, only a stabbing burn. He winced against the pain. He lifted one hand, wincing again as skin pulled against the open scratches. There was a smearing of blood and he regretted leaving his gloves in the car. It was stupid. He hadn't been prepared and that was the first rule.

David took a deep breath, scolding himself before continuing upward. For the next thirty minutes he crept up, the going only getting harder the further he ascended. The burning had given way to a dull throb. He knew he had banged his knees more than once, but there was very little feeling from his thighs down. He pushed the thought back and focused only on making his way up, on escaping.

A short time later he paused, glancing back down the mountain to where the river was four hundred feet below. There was no sign of the man following, which was good. In the condition he was in, there was no way he'd be able to outclimb the killer. He would get caught and be thrown down the mountainside into the frozen river below. That's what the man would do. He'd kill him and use the icy river to hide his body.

David shook the thought, turning his attention to a small flat area about a dozen feet above. When he reached it, he stood, catching his breath. Below the forest spread for as far as the eye could see, disappearing into an ashen horizon. It was a vast, endless expanse of grey and white with intermittent flecks of green puncturing through. The sun overhead didn't pierce the clouds, and only a brighter section of gray indicated that it was still there.

David pulled his gaze away, focusing back on the mountain. His feet still burned and his legs were caught in an icy grip, frozen needles piercing into him. He couldn't feel it, but his legs quivered under his weight. He scanned further down the outcropping and saw a small opening where the mountain disappeared inside. Just beyond, a dead tree leaned out over the edge, its dried leaves clinging to splayed wooden fingers.

He made his way towards the opening and realized it was a small cave, a den likely used by some type of animal. He didn't bother checking for tracks, but as he leaned down and stuck his face in, he found himself hoping that it was unoccupied.

"Hello?" he called out as loudly as he dared to, a raised whisper waiting for a response. When nothing came charging out, and no growl returned, David crouched down and crawled inside. The interior of the small cave was only about three feet tall, but it went back nearly twelve. To his relief, the freezing wind died out as soon as he was inside. He crawled on his hands and knees towards the back, his hands brushing against small stones and what he quickly noticed were tiny animal bones. This cave did belong, or had at one point, to something else. But at that moment all David could concern himself with was getting warm, and with the freezing wind blocked out, he crept further back.

When he reached the rear of the cave he turned, pressing his back against the wall and brought his knees up into his jacket. He pulled his arms into his sleeves and wrapped them around his folded legs. Lowering his face into the collar, David began to breath out in long, slow exhales, using his breath to warm his curled-up body. His eyes moved to the entrance of the den, staring out at the vast gray that showed beyond. He knew that somewhere down there, hidden in the woods that lay out of sight below, was the man who was hunting him, the man who had killed his father and done bad things to his mom. He missed them; his parents, and felt a deep longing welling up in his chest. He didn't know what to do. He'd learned a lot in Scouts and loved learning about survival, but sitting there frozen at the back of the cave he had completely forgotten everything he knew. The only memories that he could conjure were that of his mom and dad, and how happy they had been when they had cut down the tree. He saw their faces as they made their way down the row at the trailer park, and how they had smiled lovingly at each other. He saw his dad smiling at his mommy—mom, bundled up in the living room. He saw his dad smiling back at him from the front seat of the car and the warmth he had felt when he had told him he would teach him to shoot. He missed them so much. But he had to survive. He had to get warm so that he could make it to the top. Then he would go back down and find his mom. He would find her, and tell her that he found the way back home. Then they would escape and get the sheriff. The sheriff would arrest the man and he would go to court and the judge would kill him, just like he had killed his dad. There would be justice and his mommy and him could be happy knowing the man was dead. They would miss his dad every day. David missed him now and knew that the feeling wasn't going to go away. He just had to survive long enough.

Chapter 17

The sun crept across the sky, making its way behind the mountain ridge and taking all of its hidden warmth with it. The sky turned from slate to ash and in a matter of minutes the temperature began to plummet. The biting wind had died down, making way for the most serene, frozen quiet. The air slowly edged its way into the small cave and David lay huddled in the back, his body chilled straight to the bone. It was the kind of cold he could feel in his soul.

He was shivering, his arms and legs tucked tightly in his puffy jacket, his hands wrapped even tighter around his frozen legs, his feet below spasming and numb. Outside, the shadows crept upwards, the darkness moving to invade his tiny space.

David pulled his head from his jacket. Almost immediately his teeth began to chatter, his body trembling from the cold. He took one deep breath, the chill coating his throat, and exhaled the plume in front of him, watching the darkening sky through the cloud. He had to do something or he was going to freeze to death in this cave. He knew he would become a meal for whatever animal made it its home, and his mom would be left alone with the bad man. As he lay there with his legs trembling, his cold-clouded mind raced. He forced himself up and began the short crawl to the den's entrance.

David emerged, rising shakily to his feet. Darkness had blanketed the valley below, the pristine white now a dull blue. A dark indigo weaved its way through the clouds overhead and the horizon was somewhere beyond. He stared down, fear building up as he realized that he had no idea where he was, or which way he'd come from. He knew that if he could just get to the top, he'd be able to see the city, and if he could do that, then he might be able to go get help. The sheriffs would help. His dad had told him plenty of times, *"if you ever have an emergency, dial 911, or find a sheriff."*

As he stood there, the cold pressed in, biting through his leather snow-boots with a vengeance. He was motionless, his breath fanning outwards, two, three times. Then he turned his gaze to the dead tree just a short distance away. Moments later he was standing beneath it, pulling at the lower branches. The first few gave way easily, breaking off with a snap. The ones just above were a little more difficult, almost out of reach. He had to jump to grab onto them. With every landing his feet cried out, a thousand needles stabbing upwards. On the fourth jump he managed to wrap his hands around a larger, needle covered pine branch. He hung on, the numbness at the tip of his fingers threatening to peel his grip free. He bounced up and down twice, pulling himself up slightly and letting gravity do the rest. On the third try the branch gave way with a soft *crack* and he dropped to the ground.

David fell backwards, landing heavily on his butt, but he didn't release his grasp on the branch. He stood, picking up a handful of the smaller branches and bundling them in one arm before grabbing the larger one and dragging it back to the den. Just outside, he dropped his haul and made his way back to the tree, repeating the process. A short time later he had amassed a decent sized pile of branches and three larger ones that still had their flora attached. One by one he placed the branches against a small rock by the entrance and stomped down on them, breaking them into smaller pieces. David's feet cried out with every impact, but he clenched his jaw, wincing away the pain. He had to. A few minutes later he had a large pile of small firewood. After four trips, the wood was stacked neatly near the back of the den.

David crept back outside. Grabbing the three largest branches, he stood them up and overlapped them. Then he leaned them against the entrance and carefully slid behind, making careful not to knock them over. He sat there, staring at the make-shift door.

He knew all it would take was a single gust for the branches to be pulled away and the cold would come creeping back. He then remembered the twine in his pocket. Unzipping it, he reached in and pulled the small spool out. He unthreaded a piece about six feet in length and cut it with his knife. Afterward, he folded the blade, slid it back in his pocket and began the process of weaving the twine through the branches to bind them together. When he was finished, he tied the string in a knot and moved the now sturdier door aside, stepping back out. The sun had moved far behind the mountain and the valley below had become dark. He could see the vapor of grey just overhead, but everything else was hidden from view.

David made his way to a large rock a few feet away, pushing and pulling it towards the cave entrance. He used the last of his strength to shove it just inside. When he had finished the task, he crept back in, hoisting the bound-branch doorway back into place and used the twine to secure the flap to the large rock. That way, even if the wind managed to blow it away, it wouldn't be lost down the mountain. Afterward, he crept to the back of the cave and began arranging some of the smaller sticks into a circular pile.

He pulled from deep in his memory, wishing desperately at that moment that he hadn't left his backpack in the car. His survival guide had all the different ways to start a fire in it, but he only loosely remembered one. "Please work…" he whispered, placing one of the branches on a flat piece of the bark. For the next few minutes David rubbed it back and forth in his hands, rolling it like a playdough snake. The friction warmed his hands up to his shoulders and he could feel the burn work its way across his back. A thin sweat had worked up on his brow and a soft trickle trailed down the back of his neck. Again and again, he rolled his hands back and forth. Eventually, the smallest whisp of smoke rose up.

He looked down, pausing for the fraction of a breath, and then continued, his hands moving at twice the speed they had. The thin trail birthed more smoke, and soon there was a small glowing ember beneath. David dug furiously in his pockets, pulling the twine back out. Then he pulled a small length free, cutting it with his knife and balling it in his hands. He set the small ball of twine on top of the glowing ember and leaned down, blowing softly. A moment later the twine caught and a small shock of flame appeared. It was all David could do not to cry out in excitement. He gently placed the burning twine beneath the pile of small twigs and watched the flames creep up. A short time later he had a small fire, some of the larger sticks burning brightly atop.

David waited until the cave began to warm, which in its small confines wasn't that long. Smoke had filled the space and more than once he had taken in a lungful, sending him into a coughing fit. Yet, he realized he'd rather cough than freeze, so he used his shirt to filter the smoke when it got too thick. He removed his boots and placed them on their sides next to the fire. He pulled off his socks next and placed them atop his boots. He then removed his jacket and laid it out. Moments later he was stripped down to his underwear, his pants laid out neatly opposite him near the fire. David sat there, the warmth pushing back the ice in his feet, sending a torrent of tiny needle pricks as the feeling came back. For the next twenty minutes he defrosted, watching the dancing flames cast their shadows on the den walls. Then he pulled his jacket closer and curled up, letting his body soak in the warmth.

David had no idea how much time had passed when he startled awake in the darkness. The warmth of the fire had all but dissipated and even the embers had grown cold. He looked to the entrance of the den and could only see darkness beyond the branched doorway. Then the frigid cold hit him full force and a deep shiver racked his tiny frame. In a flash he sat up, scrambling to get his pants. As he reached over the pile of ash his body began to shake badly. He wondered how long he'd been asleep, but it didn't matter. It was still nighttime and the fire had gone out, letting the cold creep back in. He realized it must have been the biting air that had woken him.

David fumbled with his pants, his cold fingers struggling to pull them up in the confined space, and he eventually settled on falling to his back and arching up to pull them to his waist. When he managed to clasp them, he moved to his socks. A heavy relief washed over him as he picked the first up and realized that it was dry. At least the fire had lasted long enough for that. He slid the sock onto his foot and did the same with the other. He reached out, grabbing one of his boots and slid his hand inside. There was still moisture, but they were far from as saturated as they had been. He was thankful for that as he slipped them on. He pulled on his jacket, slipping his arms through the sleeves and zipping it to the top. David sat there for a moment, the cold clothing warming to his body. Then he pulled his arms and legs back in and wrapped himself up tightly. It felt like an eternity had passed before his eyes became heavy and sleep once again pulled him back.

Chapter 18

The sun had returned, casting its obfuscated glow across the valley. A shimmering layer of frost clung to everything, coating the mountain in a dazzling sparkle. There was a hint of warmth on the air, the kind of warmth that if you closed your eyes and tilted your head back you could almost feel it on your face.

At the entrance of the cave came a small scraping scratching sound and the make-shift doorway slid aside. Moments later an exhausted David stepped out. He stood there and stretched, letting the light wash over him for several seconds. He tilted his head back and let the cloud-blocked sun warm his face. Hunching his shoulders together, he brought his hands up and rubbed his arms vigorously. If he was to survive another night, he needed his backpack. That was in the valley down below. That was back at the car.

He allowed himself to stand there for just a moment longer, feeling the new day. Then he opened his eyes and looked down to the valley below. It didn't feel as cold as it had the day prior, and for that he was more than thankful. He had dressed for the cold, but the kind you went out into for a short period before returning back to the car. Not the kind you slept in. He lamented the thought of having to spend another night in the cave, so instead, turned his focus and his face back to the valley beneath.

Going back down was far easier than climbing up. With the thin frost on the slope, he was able to slide down, using his hands and feet to keep from plummeting to the bottom. More scrapes etched their way into his hands and he again despaired at leaving his gloves in the car. *Stupid.* He thought that the next time something like this happened, he would be far more prepared. He found himself hoping there would be no *next* time. By the time he stepped out onto the river's bank it was noon and the sun was directly overhead, still hiding behind a thick layer of cloud.

David eyed the river, looking up and down its length as far as he could. A short distance downstream was an area where the ice had either melted or broken away. He turned and trudged along the bank to the open space. Then he dropped to his hands and knees, pressing his lips to the freezing water and drank deeply.

He gulped the crystal-clear water, filling his mouth and swallowing, repeating the process until his stomach was full. Sitting back, he let his gaze wander to the tree line opposite the river. He wiped his hands on his pants to brush the grit and water away. As he was about to stand, a flicker of movement caught his eye.

David lowered his gaze to the moving water, waiting for the flicker to appear again. There! He saw it, a small trout, swimming in the current. His eyes grew big and a thousand thoughts pummeled him all at once. A stick. He needed a stick! He turned, rushing back to the slope and a tree that stood just at the base. He leapt up, grabbing ahold of one of the lower branches and used his weight to break it free. Holding it downward, he kicked at the smaller branches to clear them away until only a single shaft with some growth at the end was there. He pulled his pocket knife out and unfolded it, shaving the remaining growth away and whittling it into a point. Then he stood there, his spear in hand as he admired his quick work. With a smile he turned and raced back to the water.

David skidded to a stop at the water's edge, looking frantically into the small opening where the fish had been. He lifted the spear up, holding it poised in both hands and waited. Time crept by, the cold a forgotten memory in his excitement. He saw the flicker of a tail and, a moment later, the trout fell into view. David took a few seconds to calculate the trajectory and velocity as best his ten-year-old mind could. He took a deep breath and held it, plunging the spear downward.

The tip of the stick hit the water, barely making a splash as the fish instantly disappeared, swimming away at the first sign of movement from above. David stared down, pulling the spear back and waited. Another five minutes passed before he realized his arms were tired, and that the fish wouldn't be returning any time soon. It had gone further downstream. He lowered the stick, disappointment flaring for a moment before he dropped the spear to the ground at his side. Maybe he could try again later. Turning, he looked to the crossing he had used before.

A soft squelching sound rose as the snow compressed beneath David's boots. All around the woods had gone silent, frozen in place. There was no wind, no breeze, no indication at all that time was even moving forward. Only the soft crunching of his footsteps accompanied by his even softer breaths. He continued further in, passing another cluster of smaller trees when a splash of red caught his eye. *Berries!* His heart jumped and he dashed to the small shrub a few feet away. As he reached out to pick the first handful he paused. He knew that some berries could be poisonous. In his Scout guide it said never to eat berries you didn't know. He had forgotten how those looked, and his guide was in his backpack... He reached out, plucking one in lieu of the handful he was going to shove in his mouth. He held it up, analyzing it, studying it. There was nothing that indicated it would be poisonous. It looked like a cranberry. So, with waning caution, he placed the berry delicately in his mouth. His tongue moved over the waxy shape, rolling it around for a moment. Then he bit down. Almost immediately a sharp bitterness washed across his tongue, drying the inside of his mouth instantly. His face worked to a mask of disgust and he spat the berry out, holding his tongue out and wiping it on his sleeve. He bent down and scooped up a handful of snow and shoved it in his mouth, swishing it around until it melted. David spat the bitter water out, regretting his choice. He could still feel the tart sting. He stood there, his face sour, but relieved that it had only been one, and not the handful he had been wanting in his hunger.

He looked around, searching for any other sources of food. Nothing. He decided to make his way back towards the river. A short time later he stopped, reaching down to brush away the snow from where a small plant was peeking through. He plucked one of the leaves and placed it in his mouth. The result was not all too dissimilar to the berry, but he managed to choke it down, following it up with a second. The third proved to be too much and he spat it out, continuing on.

He had made it almost all the way back to the river when a lone howl rose up into the air. The sound stopped him in his tracks. *Wolf!* He thought, his head whipping all around him at once. The howl had sounded distant, but the way sound traveled in the frozen woods, it could have been miles away or just behind the next tree.

David stood there, lifting his beanie up to expose his ears. He listened intently, his ears moving back and forth as he struggled to hear any sounds. For the next few moments, he stayed silent, his breath held in his lungs. Nothing. He exhaled heavily and started back towards the river as quickly as he could without running. As desperately as the panic pleaded for him to charge into a full sprint, he needed to stay reserved and alert. He knew if he ran that it would obscure his ability to hear anything coming from behind.

It was a short time later that he emerged from the trees back on the bank of the river, not far from the narrow crossing. He stood there, the sound of the river flowing beneath the ice bringing him something almost akin to comfort. As he made his way back across, he was careful to better judge his leap to the last stone.

David reached spear and hoisted it up, standing there for the next few minutes, waiting for the silver shimmer of a meal. But nothing was there, only the ripples of the water moving past and the stones blurred by the current beneath. He needed his bag, but something kept him from going back for it. He knew he needed it, but he could still see the man's face in his mind and that fear kept him from venturing further.

David stayed by the water for a little while longer before taking another drink and making his way back up. He'd decided to try and make the shelter more accommodating by adding more branches to the entrance. He needed more firewood if he was going to keep the fire going throughout the night, and his arms and hips were sore from sleeping directly on the stone floor. He wanted to at least try to make some type of a bed. He smiled knowing that was something he had experience in. His troop had gone out twice. Primitive camping. They had to build their own shelter out of tree branches and use loose foliage; leaves and pine needles, to make a bed they could lie atop. He had made a really nice hut and had piled up almost six inches of debris on the floor. It hadn't been as comfortable as a real bed, but it was far better than sleeping directly on the ground. The only thing he realized, however, was that this had been in August when it was still warm outside, even at night. Now, he's in a cave on the side of the mountain in winter. He wasn't sure if it would matter how nice he made it, but he had to try. He didn't want to spend another night freezing on the ground. He didn't want to spend another night there at all.

It was a little over an hour later that David had not only made it back to the den, but had stripped a good handful of branches from two of the trees nearby. He broke and piled the sticks for firewood and stripped as many of the branches as he could of their needles. Those he dragged to the back of the cave and laid out. He piled the firewood beside it. He knew it was going to be another difficult attempt at getting the fire going and his hands hurt just thinking about it. He had two blisters on his palms from the night prior and didn't look forward to those breaking. He hated the stinging that would be there. But he didn't have a choice. After long deliberation, he didn't think he should try and return to the car so soon. The killer might still be there, or close by. Even if he did go back, he had no idea how to drive if he got there. And he didn't want to see his dad like that again. He wasn't ready. The image flashed past and he quickly shook it away, refocusing on breaking the sticks down.

He sat in the cave for the next few hours, his mind wandering through memories. Outside the sky turned through its shifting hues. He felt the air getting colder and a small breeze had begun to work past. It wouldn't be long before darkness fell over the mountain once more, but at least this time, he was a little better prepared. He reached down, pressing into the three-inch-thick pile of bedding he had created, grateful that cold stone wasn't pressing into him. He had used a handful of rocks to create a makeshift fire pit and had his small tipi of kindling ready. Beside him was the stick and bark piece he had used before.

He sat there, daydreaming and waiting. He couldn't wait to get back home and tell his friends about the adventure, about building a shelter and hunting for food, about surviving. He imagined their faces as he told the story and how the scout leader would react. He wondered what badges he would earn and knew that for sure, Tommy Jenkins had never done anything like this before. He imagined how proud his parents... The fantasies faded, a deep sadness coursing in as he thought about his parents. His dad wouldn't be proud because he was dead. *Daddy. I'm sorry.*

He could still try and rescue his mommy. *Mommy. Daddy.* It had only been the year prior that he had begun to train himself to call his parents by their grown-up names. *Mom and Dad.* Only *little* kids said mommy and daddy. It had only taken one teasing from a classmate to solidify that. But at that moment, that's who he missed. It wasn't his mother and father, or mom and dad. He missed his mommy, and the thought of his daddy lying dead in the snow, all the blood… Tears forced their way out of his eyes and in a single breath he was sobbing, his legs curled up to his chest as he rocked back and forth.

"Mommy, I miss you. Please. Please. Why did you have to die, Daddy, why?! Why did he do that? Mommy please. Please be okay. Please!" David wailed, the sound echoing inside the small confines of the den. He didn't care if he was loud, didn't even care if the killer heard him. He missed his mommy and daddy worse than he ever had. He needed their safety, their comfort. But that was gone, and now he was alone on the mountain, hungry and tired, scared and cold. He knew his mommy would know what to do. She would get them back home. He had to find her first. He had to help her get away from the man. As he sat there, tears pouring in streams down his face, he decided that's what he needed to do. He needed to get to the top of the mountain and find the way home. Then he needed to go back down and find a way to rescue his mommy. Then they could escape. Mommy knew how to drive. They just needed to get back to the car and they could go home. She would send the sheriffs and the man would go to jail.

David sat there, the sobbing done, but the tears still flowing. He stared out of the entrance to the den at the sky beyond, steeling himself. *Tomorrow. Tomorrow I'll go to the top of the mountain. Then I can see where the city is. Then. Then I'll come help you, Mommy. I promise.*

He lifted his hands, wiping the tears away and then reached out to pick up the stick and piece of bark, getting to work on building his fire.

Chapter 19

A thin layer of powder covered the Connor family car, the light gold paint of the wagon just barely visible beneath the snow.

"Help me, David. Help me."

"Mommy?" David asked, stepping slowly around the car.

The air around him was still, the forest deathly quiet. Each step he made as he edged forward crunched loudly, echoing through the woods. Atop the car the tree he had picked was withered and dry, the twine now broken and frayed, dangling limply off the car's roof.

"Please, David..."

"Mommy, I'm here," he replied, edging around the front of the car.

Lying just feet away, mouth open and gaping was his father. Blood was flowing from the frown gouged into his neck and bubbles formed where he struggled to breath.

"Daddy..." David whimpered.

"David, please. Help me."

He tore his gaze away from his father. Just a short distance away, seated in the snow with her back to him was his mother. "Mommy!" he shouted, running forward.

His legs plowed through the snow, but it pushed back. Every step was stifled, the snow thick and unmoving. He trudged through, the coldness biting into his legs. Beneath that his feet had gone numb, icy appendages frozen to his ankles. He pushed forward regardless, swinging his arms wildly in an attempt to gain momentum. An eternity passed before his reached his mom. When he reached out, his hand finally grasping her shoulder, she spun, her eyes wide and black, her mouth open in a silent scream. *"DAVID!!!"*

David shot awake, a terrified yelp escaping his lips as he pushed backwards against the cave wall. His eyes darted back and forth, his mother's face still piercing back. Then the darkness drew into view, a small glow of embers from the circle of stones. Just beyond the doorway he could see the moonlight shining silver through the clouds.

"Mommy," he whimpered, and the tears began again. He sat there, curled into himself. The feeling of sadness and loss beat at him. *She isn't dead, she isn't dead*, he kept repeating over and over in his mind. "She isn't dead. Please."

Minutes passed before the chill worked its way in. David reached out and placed another pile of sticks on the smoldering embers. He leaned forward, blowing softly on them until the flame jumped to life and the sticks caught. Then he sat back, folded his legs up and watched the glow fill the cave.

It had been two years prior that his parents had rented a cabin up the mountain. They'd gone there a week before Christmas. His father worked in the restaurant industry and that meant no holidays, so instead, they celebrated everything early. The cabin they had rented had a small metal fireplace in the corner and it had been the first year David had been allowed to be in charge of keeping the fire going. There of course, his dad had just used a lighter to get it going, but David had become a master of keeping the flames up. A little blow to heat the embers, wait for the flames to catch and then add smaller pieces before the bigger ones. He sat there, watching the tiny flames dance upwards, thinking about that Christmas, and the presents, and happiness shared. Tears worked their way sideways down his cheeks as the flames danced in his eyes. All he could feel was sadness, a great hole in his chest that burned in a sour way. He felt the hollow shivers not brought on by cold, but an unimaginable loss. He couldn't fathom how it would be on Christmas this year, or any after. His mind tried, but kept settling back on those of past. He swallowed dryly, another tear forming at the corner of his eye. A small sniffle escaped as he watched an ember pop into the air with a small *snap*.

Chapter 20

The sun had already risen above the horizon by the time David awoke the next day. He didn't know what time it was; he'd never liked wearing a watch, except for the one his daddy had given him for his birthday that was also a calculator. He only wore that when he went to school. But he had learned how to tell what time it was by where the sun was in the sky. Straight up overhead was noon, and depending on if it was summer or winter, he could guess roughly, within the hour to what time it was. Maybe nine-o'clock he guessed, wiping the sleep from his eyes as he let his gaze work to the forest below.

He swallowed hard, grimacing at the feel of his mouth. It had been two days since he had last brushed his teeth and he could taste it. Brush twice a day and floss after every meal. He didn't have a lot of routines, but that was one. Some of the other kids had braces and he saw how much they hated it. And he had no desire to be called brace-face for three years, so oral hygiene was it for him. That was one of the things he took seriously.

The sky overhead had cleared considerably. The grey was nearly white and patches of light blue peeked through in spots. The sun was already beginning to melt the thin layer of frost that had been left the night before. He took in the valley below, then upward to the mountain ridge a short distance above. He was happy that the air was only slightly chilly and that he was fully dried from the fall in the river before. The clouds overhead allowed for a gentle warmth to beam down from above. For the next few moments he stood there, soaking it in. Then with one deep breath, David stretched, the motion turning to a yawn, gave himself a small shake and started hiking.

The way up was a frost-covered path of loose shale and wet limestone. Every step shifted beneath David's feet. There were small handholds and gnarled roots sticking out of the mountainside that kept him from sliding back down, but more than a few times the footing beneath him had given way, sending a small landslide of pebbles and baseball sized stones clattering downward. His stomach grumbled angrily and he could feel that he had far less energy than he normally did. He could feel the sharp pains of hunger piercing his gut. Further up the air seemed crisper, but it also he seemed to take deeper breaths in order to get the air he needed. On more than one occasion he stopped, taking in as much of the cool air as he could to catch his breath. It was like yawning without that last little bit to make it satisfying. He kept pushing on, following the thinning ravine upward.

Nearly an hour had passed before David looked up to see the ridge's summit just a short distance away. He stopped, catching his breath for the hundredth time and turned, looking back down. The height was dizzying. The distant trees below all blended into a patchwork of white and he could see the range far beyond that. The sky had continued to clear and more faint patches of blue pierced through. The cold air seemed to lift upward, moving past him to reach the top. For a moment he sat there, his feet dug into the terrain as his eyes scanned the forest below him. He was looking for the small clearing, for his parent's car, for any sign of where the killer could be, but only a blanket of white lay was in sight; a collage of frozen pines and firs.

He allowed time for his breath to catch up and the heartbeat pounding in his neck to mellow before turning and continuing to the top. A few minutes later David was pulling himself up to a small flat area above. He hadn't taken more than two steps when the ground beneath his feet gave way and he was sent sliding down towards the edge of the slope. He struggled to stop himself, kicking out and reaching to grasp anything that moved past. The slope was steep and he was picking up speed the farther he slid. In a desperate attempt to gain control he managed to roll over, sliding down on his stomach. The jagged rocks caught his jacket, lifting it up around his chest and digging sharply into his stomach, leaving deep scrapes as they gouged into his skin. His hand grasped a small root sticking out and as his body weight yanked against it, it pulled free, showering him with dirt. He continued sliding, still picking up speed when he slid right into a fallen tree, his body impacting heavily against it.

David lay there for a moment, struggling to catch the breath that was knocked from his chest. He gasped, the pressure crushing him. He forced past it and took a lungful of air, but lay there for the next few moments, his adrenaline slowly melting away. He turned his head to see the large log he had slammed against. With a pained wince, he dragged his body up and froze. The tree was right in front of him, but there was nothing beyond that, just a vast, empty sky and the valley hundreds of feet below. David placed his hands on the edge of the log and carefully leaned over.

Just beyond the fallen tree was a sheer cliff, dropping nearly three hundred feet to where the slope continued downward. A massive granite rock wall plunged straight into a great pile of boulders and debris below. David pulled back, falling to a seated position. If that tree hadn't been there, he would have nosedived right off the edge of the cliff to his death. He sat there, his heart pounding in his chest before he turned and started carefully making his way back up to the ridge. He had to keep going.

By the time David clamored back to the ridge he was tired and out of breath. His whole body hurt and he could feel the stinging of the cuts along his stomach and chest. His hands were bleeding and there was a steady throbbing where one of his knees had struck solidly against a rock on the way down.

He took a moment to lift his jacket and shirt and check the damage. Deep scratches and cuts covered his skin. He lowered his shirt, wincing as he pressed his hand against his chest. He'd need to clean that and he knew that meant getting cold and wet again. He put that thought off, something to worry about when he got back down to the river. For now, he turned his attention to the reason he had climbed to the top in the first place. He had to get his bearings.

"If you ever get lost in the woods, either find a stream or river that leads down and follow it. Or, climb as far up as you can to the top and try and get your bearings that way."

David's Scout leader's words echoed in his ears and his face pulled tight as he turned to make his way to the tip of the peak a few hundred feet away. A short time later he crested the peak, finding a large flat area at the top. He stood there, catching his breath once more and looked around.

David's mouth fell open as his gaze worked across the vision before. The entire climb he had preoccupied himself with the thought of seeing the city in the distance, and how long it would take him to get there on foot. He was hoping he could be there by the end of the day. What he couldn't have known however, was that they had driven close to an hour to get to the logging road, and that it had been from the opposite direction. David stood facing west, an endless swath of tree-dotted plain spreading out to the horizon. The city they lived in was behind him, to the east, with another mountain ridge and just over thirty miles separating them.

He stood there, staring into the vast wilderness and felt his heart sink. What little remainder of hope he had sapped away, leaving him scared and alone. There would be no sheriff, no rescue, no hot chocolate. All he would get was more cold and more alone.

The icy air brushed past him, tugging at the sleeves of his jacket as it moved past and continued down the opposite side of the slope. A hollow hopelessness dug into him, the disappointment heavy and thick. He stood there blankly, not even tears forming in his eyes. He was lost and realized right then just how desperate his situation was. Somewhere below the *murderer* was still hunting him. Somewhere below his mother was still scared, the bad man doing bad things to her. Maybe if he could stay alive long enough, someone would come looking for them. He'd seen TV shows where people go missing and they send out search parties and helicopters. Maybe they would do that for them. Someone had to know they hadn't come back. He also knew it had only been two days, and both of his parents had taken the weekend off, so it wouldn't be another day or two until someone realized they were missing.

David stood there, the weight of his situation pummeling him. He was helpless and alone. There was nothing else he could do except return to his hideout. He turned and started his descent when a single strand of smoke caught his eye.

Deep in the valley below a thin tendril of gray rose to the sky. A campfire. David stared, watching as the smoke lifted and disappeared into the air above. Just beyond he saw where a narrow line cut through the trees. He traced that line through the woods, following to where it led to another part of the mountain further beyond, leading downward before disappearing. He swallowed hard, piecing it together. That thin line had to be the road they had used coming in. The mountain was the one they had made their way up. If he could just get to that road, he could get back to town.

His eyes moved back to the smoke. Cold dread clamped hold of him, his stomach twisting into a knot. Another small grumble escaped as his hunger cried out. His hands moved to his stomach while he stared down in thought. If the man had gone back to his camp, then that meant that he might not be at his parent's car anymore. He could get his backpack. Then he'd have his survival book and his gloves. And food. They hadn't eaten lunch yet. That meant there were three sandwiches, bananas and sodas there. He just had to get to them. So, David swallowed hard again, his stomach rumbling loudly once more, and started his way down the peak, this time a lot more carefully.

Chapter 21

David knelt by the river, his jacket and shirt folded on the ground behind him. He readied himself, taking a few deep breaths before plunging his hand in the icy water and scooping a large handful out and splashing it against his chest. A small cry escaped as he rubbed the frozen liquid over his cuts. He repeated the process a few more times, gritting his teeth as he brushed the small pieces of rock and dirt that had lodged itself into the abrasions. When he finished, he stood and made his way back to his clothing, using the shirt to carefully dab his chest and stomach dry before slipping it over his head and putting his jacket on. He then turned his attention to the woods beyond.

The ice had melted off the rocks he had used to cross, making it easier and quicker to get to the other side. Moments later he was following the trail he'd left two days prior.

David retraced his steps, trying his best to follow his earlier tracks. He knew that the killer had been able to track him because of it, so he decided that instead of creating new ones and potentially giving away that he had returned, that he would simply trace the others. He'd seen it in a movie one time with a boy his age in a really scary hotel. He remembered Mommy getting really upset because Daddy had let him watch it. He had gotten nightmares for a week because of that, and every time his mother would yell at his father.

"I told you; you shouldn't have let him watch that! What the hell were you thinking?"

"You'd never try to hurt me like that? Would you dad?"

"No kiddo," his dad had replied, smiling. "It's just a movie."

"Okay. But I don't ever want to go to that hotel."

"Trust me," his dad had said. "We're not going to Colorado any time soon."

And they hadn't. They'd gone to New Mexico later that year and to Arizona the next. His mother had a fascination with Native American jewelry and had finally convinced his dad to take her there. They never went to Colorado and never stayed at the scary hotel.

David followed the trail, lost in thought when a sound ripped him out of the memories. He jerked his gaze away from the two sets of footprints below and snapped his head to the trees. Standing just twenty feet away was a large white-tailed deer. He stood there, staring, fear turning to awe as he watched the creature slowly lift its head. Two big eyes locked to him and he watched as its ears twitched back and forth. A smile pulled at his cheeks. With a flash of its tail, it turned and bound away into the trees.

"Cool," he whispered, staring into the empty space for a moment longer before continuing on. He followed the trail, watching as the bigger prints left by the man followed along with his. A short while later, the trees fell away and he slowed to a stop. Just ahead, tree still bound on top, was their gold Town & Country station wagon.

David felt the air leave his lungs. A dark dread filled him, a dull panic flaring just behind. Slowly he stepped forward, edging his way towards the front of the car. As he crept forward, he noticed that the tires were flat. Deep gashes were in the sidewalls of each one where a knife had been plunged in. The killer had slashed the tires to keep anyone from escaping.

Slowly, he edged his way around the car. And then the full scene fell into view. Lying in the same place he had when David had run, was his father. A fine layer of snow covered his daddy's corpse, the bluish-white of his skin showing through. Crimson was splashed outwards, so much more blood than David had remembered seeing. A deep hole in the snow surrounded his daddy's upper body like a dark, crimson halo. He swallowed heavily, yanking his gaze away to the other body lying in the snow. Just ten feet away was his mother. She was lying on her back and he could see where her clothes had been torn off. Her skin didn't seem real, like it was made of plastic and the color was wrong. Blood surrounded the body and he could see the deep, visceral gashes where she had been stabbed multiple times in the chest. A single, deep gash ran across her neck and for the flicker of an instant he thought he saw bone inside. David stood there, paralyzed in a terrible loss as the reality of it all plummeted into him. Both of his parents were dead. Daddy *and* Mommy. There was no rescuing her, no getting back to the car and escaping, no going home and no sheriff. He was alone and the *murderer* was still out there in the woods.

Tears poured down his cheeks as he pulled his gaze painfully away. Almost robotically, he made his way to the car, opening the back door and reaching in. He pulled his backpack towards him, unzipping it. Then he took the lunch bag that was on the floor of the backseat and opened it, pulling one of the bananas out and setting it aside. He placed the lunch bag inside of his backpack. Then he slid his gloves over his hands, tears still falling as he quietly mumbled his fears to himself and lifted the banana, slowly peeling it before taking the first bite. He wasn't hungry, not anymore. His stomach was nauseous and he felt like throwing up, but it also hurt. He hadn't eaten in two days and had never felt that kind of hunger before. So he forced it down, bit by bit, one bite at a time until it was gone. Then he dropped the peel next to the car and stepped back, closing the door.

"Well, lookie here."

David spun, nearly losing his footing. Standing thirty feet away at the edge of the clearing was the man who'd killed both his parents.

"You done come back to check on your folks, did ya?"

David stared, his face warping in horror.

"Yeah," the man continued as he glanced around. "Kinda figured you would. All alone, surrounded by these *big, scary* woods."

David was frozen. He was too scared to speak, too scared to run. All he could do was stare in horrid terror at the man across glaring at him.

"Sorry about your mama," the man continued with a smirk as his gaze moved to his mother's frozen body. "I sure would have loved to keep her around a while." He paused, looking back to David. "She didn't much like that idea none." He smiled. "She don't seem to have a problem with it now though. Sticking around, I mean."

David felt heat rising in him.

"Now there's the matter of what I'm s'posed to do with you."

David shoved past the fear, one foot slowly edging sideways.

The man flinched forward, a *snarl* escaping. David froze once more. The man grinned, a foul gesture betraying his intentions. "I really am sorry. But I can't have no loose ends running around, trying to get themselves rescued. Wouldn't be too convenient for me, the law finding out what it is I do out here." He paused, his gaze narrowing in on David. "I want you to know, I take no pleasure in this, but it's gotta be done, so we might as well get this over with."

David willed his feet to move, one foot shifting outwards as he edged towards the front of the car.

Across the clearing the man watched with mild amusement as the young boy slowly slid the straps of his backpack into place.

David took another step, his eyes never leaving the other. He'd escaped once, but he had also had a long head start. He knew he wasn't going to get far this time, but he had to try. He took another step, his back sliding against the cold metal side of the car.

"Well," the man said, the sickly smile tearing at his cheeks. "Go on then. Run."

David turned, darting back around the car and charging as fast as he could through the snow. Thankfully the path had already been cut twice, so he was able to run full speed without having to worry about what his feet would catch on.

"Run boy!" the man shouted from behind. "I gots nothing but time."

David continued running as fast as his feet would allow.

"We'll see how long you last out there," the man's voice echoed out from behind.

Back in the clearing the smile dropped from the man's face, a cruel malice pulling his features taught. "If the cold and hunger don't kill you, I will."

David continued forward, barreling through the trees.

Branches reached out and slapped him in the face as he ran past. A thin pink line was marked across his forehead and from there a single drop of blood worked its way down. His lungs were already ablaze, but adrenaline kept his momentum. He passed a small cluster of trees, following the trail as quickly as he could. The next few minutes blurred past as he struggled to keep his pace. Fear had left him drained and he could feel exhaustion creeping in. He felt himself beginning to slow. Then thirty feet away the man stepped out from behind a tree, large clouds of breath swelling outward.

"Hey!" the man shouted, his lungs heaving in and out of breath.

David screamed, dashing off the trail into the trees. He kept his mental compass, running towards what he hoped was the mountain. It was easy to get turned around when all you could see surrounding you were trees and snow.

Behind him the killer took a moment to lean against a tree and catch his breath. He reached into his jacket pocket, pulling out a pack of cigarettes and a lighter, lighting one up and taking a deep drag. "Jesus," He growled, taking another puff before starting after the boy at a walking pace.

David continued running. Once again, his legs were weak and he was out of breath, his lungs burning with each breath and there was a thin layer of fog in his head from the exhaustion and onset of malnutrition lingering ever so close. Just then, right beyond the trees he saw the river. He pushed himself faster, running to the tree line and stepping out onto the bank. His head whipped back and forth until spied the ridgeline a hundred yards away. He turned and started up. He'd made it about twenty yards when the man emerged from the trees behind, calling out to him. "Forgot about that river didn't you!"

David paused, looking back over his shoulder to see the man standing there with a smile.

"Bet you're getting *real* hungry by now," the man called out, pulling a bag of jerky from his pocket. The man pulled a piece out and popped it into his mouth. "You go on and keep runnin boy! Eventually you're gon' get tired. And when you do, I'm gon' be right there!"

David turned and darted back into the trees. He could see the crossing a good distance away and knew he couldn't lead the man there. If he got caught on the mountain, he'd have nowhere to go except up. And if the man chased him to the top...

The man started after, following the boy at a casual pace. He didn't need to run. The boy was going to eventually tire himself out. It was cold, and he was hungry. He knew it wouldn't be long before the boy either collapsed or gave up. All he needed to do was follow behind, keep to the tracks, and eventually he'd get his hands on him. Then he'd tie up loose ends and head back to camp. He'd been meaning to move spots anyways. Hell. He was gonna leave the day prior cept' for the snow. He was just gonna wait long enough for it to clear up before he broke down camp and moved on to the next spot. Somewhere further north, he'd been thinking. Wyoming maybe. Lots of open country. Lots of small towns and unlocked doors. He'd been craving himself some good ole country girl for a while.

As he followed nonchalantly he played around with the different ways of taking care of business. This would be his first time with a kid, and though he didn't find any sexual desires in it, the thought lingered just in the background. Maybe... *Don't knock it till you try it* he'd always said. Maybe he'd toy with him for a bit, see what kind of scrap he had in him. Maybe he'd let him think he was getting the upper hand and then, *bam!* He'd wrap his hands around his neck and squeeze until his little face turned purple and his eyes bulged out of his skull. Or maybe he'd see how long it took the brat to freeze to death in the icy creek. That could be fun, just dip him in, lowering him slowly till the cold took him. Wouldn't have to worry about disposing of the body, he thought. Let the creek do the work.

David ran through the trees, zig-zagging and doing what he could to make a mess of his trail. He'd circled around twice and even stopped to walk backwards for a bit. Overhead the sky had begun to darken and a light flurry began to fall. He ran for another ten minutes before cutting back towards the river. A few minutes later he reached the edge of the trees.

He leaned out, looking back downstream. It was clear. That meant the man was still following his trail behind, but he also knew that it meant he wasn't far either. The crossing was only ten yards away and he turned, darting towards it. Then he slid to a stop, turning to look behind him. It was too easy.

David ran back to where he had left the trees and turned around, taking large, spread-out steps as he walked backwards through the snow. He turned and kept going for about a hundred feet before stopping and retracing his steps. Then he repeated the process a few yards further, making his way out and then into a circle before returning. He'd seen a movie once where a man wearing large snowshoes had done the same and it had thrown the men following him off his trail. He once again followed his steps out and then ran as fast as he could to the crossing, leaping across, panic not allowing for care as he bound from stone to stone to the other side. Then moments later he was scrambling up the ravine.

Back in the woods the man was following the tracks. He smiled as he saw them cut back into the trees and turned to follow. He walked for another few minutes till the tracks came to a stop. For a moment he stood there, his gaze working over the untouched snow around. With a growl he turned, starting back, irritation chafing him.

David continued upwards, trying desperately to not dislodge any loose stones. He was ascending quickly, familiar handholds falling into place. It took him twenty minutes to reach the small outcropping and as he did he turned, looking back down the mountain. He was ready to see the man climbing up, that terrible smile splitting his face. But there was no one there. He scanned the trees, his gaze moving to the river. Then he saw the man step out, his head moving back and forth as he scanned the river's edge.

David dropped down, lying flat and pressing his body as far down as he possibly could. He knew the man's gaze would work its way up the mountain and he desperately hoped the small ledge concealed him enough. For the next short while he lay there, his face pressed against the cool mountainside. Then he slowly leaned up and risked a look.

Below the riverbank was empty. The man had either given up or gone back to retrace his steps. He knew that the loops and backtracking would confuse him for a while. That's all it needed to do, just give him enough time to climb back up the mountain and into the den. After watching for a few minutes longer, David jumped up and rushed to the small cave, scrambling inside.

He pulled the door closed, crawling quickly to the back and pressing his body against the wall. He slowly removed his pack and set it next to him, his eyes glued to the entrance. For the next hour he sat motionless, fear coursing through him. When he managed to convince himself that he hadn't been followed, he opened up his pack and pulled one of the sandwiches out.

Slowly, he removed the sandwich from the plastic wrapper, lifting the top piece of bread away. Double thick ham and cheese. No mayo. It was his mom's. He forced back a small sob and shoved the first bite into his mouth, nearly choking from swallowing after only chewing twice. He forced himself to slow down and sat there silently, finishing the last of the sandwich.

David reached into the bag and pulled a can of soda out, cracking it open and taking a big sip. He felt the cool carbonation fizzle down his throat and let a small burp escape. "Scuse me," he said softly, habit forming the words followed by the realization that there was no point. He took another sip and set the can down.

David pulled his survival book out and squinted though the darkness at it before flipping it open and beginning his studies. For the next three hours he sat there and absorbed as much information as he could. Bow drills, figure-four traps, deadfall traps. He studied the diagrams and read each passage three times, a trick his mother had taught him in the fourth grade. It helped with re… retend… Retention! It helped him remember better.

Outside the sky fell dark. The day's events had left David completely drained. He was curled up against the back wall, his legs and arms tucked into his dirty jacket. He hadn't had the energy to start a fire, and even if he had, his hands were far too sore. He folded himself up into the jacket once more and let the throbbing exhaustion pull him away.

Chapter 22

Snow continued to fall into the night, the flakes growing larger as they covered everything in a fresh coating of powder. Just outside of the cave, a low hanging blanket of white and grey hovered beyond, its frozen contents continuing to empty soundlessly onto the valley below. David slept soundly, his tiny snores rising out of the jacket. Inside he was still cozy, though the familiar chill began to nip at his feet. He shifted slightly, a small sound pulling him from sleep.

Just feet away, inside the cave was a shifting sound. He tensed, knowing he'd been found, but frantically hoped that if he stayed impossibly still he wouldn't be seen. His eyes darted back and forth in the darkness of his jacket as the rustling crept closer. It stopped, and then a sound torn from the most terrifying nightmare rang, a low rumble of breath followed by a visceral hiss. He stayed frozen. Whatever it was that lived here had returned.

David held his breath, his eyes widened in terror. A dark, malevolent shape shifted and turned beside him. Another low growl was followed by deep, wet hissing sound. He stayed frozen. He couldn't look, he couldn't move. Even when the breath could no longer stay hidden in his lungs, he didn't move. He aimed his breathing downwards, towards his legs and released it slowly and steadily.

He could feel the creature's presence. David waited for the ripping claws and gnashing teeth, for the terrible scream whatever monster was approaching would release upon attack, but nothing came. Only another low growl followed by silence. Time ceased to exist inside his jacket, the seconds stretching minutes and the minutes becoming days. He struggled to keep still, struggled against the exhaustion trying to reel him back, and as he lay there silently and unmoving, he let his thoughts wander back to his home.

* * *

"David, come on! We have to go or we're gonna be late."

"But I don't wanna go. Nobody's gonna be there anyways."

David looked across the living room to where his mom stood, her gaze locked onto him. It had been his birthday, and she was doing her best to coax him out of the house. That was not what he had wanted. His best friend had moved away just a few months prior and he knew she was just trying to get him out of the house for some stupid surprise birthday party at the diner his dad worked at. They'd done the same thing the year before.

"We have to pick your dad up from work. I needed the car this morning and he doesn't have a ride home. So, get your jacket on and let's go."

"Mom. I'm not stupid. I know we're just going there because it's my birthday."

"David…"

"No one's gonna be there. Ben moved to Arizona and Caleb's in San Francisco with his family. It's just gonna be me and it's embarrassing!"

"Oh. I'm sorry," his mom replied, her face scrunching up. "You're embarrassed to be seen with your parents now?"

"No…" Now he did truly feel embarrassed. "I didn't-I'm sorry."

"Look. Your dad and I both know how hard it's been on you losing Ben. Trust me, we do. We may just be your parents, but don't forget we also had a life before you came along. Your dad and I had to grow up, too. We also know what it's like to lose a good friend. But I can promise you, you have more friends than you think."

David's gaze dropped to the floor.

"Look, if you wanna spend your birthday moping around the house feeling sorry for yourself, then that's entirely your prerogative.

We aren't going to stop you. That doesn't change the fact that we still have to go pick your father up from work. So please, David. Go put your jacket on so we can go."

David turned, returning to his room for his jacket. By the time he got back to the living room his mom was already outside, the car's engine running. He opened the car door and stepped in, his gaze locked on the trailer as she backed out and started down the lane.

The entire drive to the restaurant he was quiet. It was the first birthday in three years he wouldn't be spending with his best friend. Ben Dean had been the coolest kid he'd ever met, and from the moment they sat together at lunch they knew they would be best friends. For the last three years they had been, hanging out almost every day. Ben had been the one to get him into Scouts. And then his dad had taken a job in Arizona. Two months later they left and he was gone. David had other friends, but the kind he only spoke to at school. The last few months it had been Scouts, then home, then games. He didn't even want to go outside to play anymore. He'd go out, look at his bike and feel nothing but sadness. There would be no trail riding with Ben or building jumps. It had lost all the magic.

David's gaze was locked to the dashboard in front of him as they pulled into the restaurant driveway. It was only when the car was parked that he lifted his gaze.

"Come on grumpy bear," his mom said, tapping his leg before getting out.

David stepped out of the car and followed his mom. He instinctively scanned the windows of the restaurant, looking for balloons or other telltale signs of the impending surprise party. But he didn't' see anything. A small part of him felt disappointed.

"Come on," his mom repeated as she opened the door, holding it for him.

He stepped in, scanning the inside. No balloons, no smiling faces, no *'surprise'* yelled. He felt his face drop.

"Go grab a seat," his mom said, gesturing to a booth a few feet away. "I've gotta use the bathroom. Your dad should be out in a minute."

David nodded, walking towards the booth as a sadness drew in to accompany his steps.

He slid into the booth, taking one last look around before letting his gaze fall to the menu he'd looked at a hundred times before.

"BOO!"

David flinched to the side, jerking backwards at the noise. Then, recognition hit and his face lit up like a Christmas tree. "NO WAY!"

Standing at the edge of the booth with a smile stretched from ear to ear was his best friend, Ben.

"Surprise!"

David leapt out of the booth, pulling his best friend into a huge embrace. Only then did he see the door behind him open up and a dozen other kids come piling in, his dad right behind with a huge grin on his face.

David released his friend and stepped back as the entire Scout troop made their way towards him, balloons and presents in hand. All of that was secondary to having his best friend there.

"I thought you were in Arizona!"

"My dad had to come back for a week for work. I'm being homeschooled so he brought me with him."

"You're gonna be here for a week!?"

"Yep! Hope you still have air in your tires."

"Surprise!"

David turned to see his mom standing there, a warm smile on her face. She grinned at Ben and then turned her attention back to him. "We spoke with Ben's father a few weeks ago. He'd called checking in on you, to see how you were doing and to let us know he'd be in town for a week. We figured Ben could come stay with us while his dad focuses on his work. I mean, if that's alright with you."

David was at a loss for words, overcome with emotion. He rushed forward, embracing his mom tightly. "Thank you."

Cheryl leaned down, brushing her fingers through his hair and smiling.

"Dude! Wait till you see what I got you for your birthday," Ben smiled, holding out a small package that would contain the coolest pocket knife he'd ever seen.

The rest of the party was amazing. David spent it surrounded by his friends. He'd opened his presents, eaten cake and shared countless laughs, but the best present he could have gotten was having his best friend back. Even if it had only been for a week, it was the best week he'd ever had.

* * *

Lying there in the cold darkness of the cave, David's hand moved to the knife in his pocket. He thought about his friend. They'd only been in contact a few times after that, school and Scouts pulling his attention away slowly over the next two years. Now he only thought about his friend every so often. This just happened to be one of those moments.

David lay there in the dark, his memories pulling him away as sleep grasped his thoughts. It was only a short time later that the silent exhaustion dragged him back into the darkness of his dreams.

Chapter 23

Tiny ripples moved beneath the dirty bundle of cloth, a faint yawn escaping from within. A moment later two small boots edged outward, followed by painfully cramped legs. The muscles in David's legs groaned as he released his legs from the jacket shell they'd been tucked into the entire night. The rest of his body drew rigid in a stiff stretch, his folded arms squeezing tightly against his chest. Then he brought his arms up, sliding them through the sleeves, his face emerging a moment later from the top.

He lay there for a moment, his eyes dry and crusted, staring at the rock lines above. Then he remembered. His eyes shot open as he jerked to the side. The den was empty, save for himself, and for a moment wondered if what he had heard the night prior had been his imagination or a dream. David carefully brought himself up to a seated position, his legs still stretched out in front. He eyed the rest of the small den cautiously before reaching over and pulling his pack close. Then he reached in, pulled one of the two remaining bananas out and peeled the top down. For the next few minutes, he sat in silence, quietly chewing his rationed breakfast. The second sandwich would have to wait until later, when he was really hungry, and even then, he was only going to allow himself half. What little food he had needed to last. It could be days until he figured out how to get back to town or was rescued.

David finished the banana and leaned forward, gently tossing the peel into the fire ring. He zipped his bag and slung it across his back before crawling to the door. A fresh coating of powder had fallen overnight, less than an inch. The makeshift door moved outward slightly before sliding aside and the small boy climbed out.

As he stood there and observed the valley below something at his feet caught his eye. He looked down, a large yawn creeping from his lips as the markings below registered. Tracks. David stared down at them, memory working against the sleepiness that still wrapped his thoughts. He slid one arm out of a strap and slung his pack forward, unzipping it and carefully removing his book. He let the bag hand loosely from one arm as he opened and thumbed through the book. When he came to the section showing the different animal prints that were most commonly found, he held it out, doing his best to match it to the ones below. It didn't take long before the fresh tracks in the snow matched a set in the book. Bobcat.

David lowered the book, his eyes following the tracks as they made their way past the two trees and further up the slope. He returned his book back to his bag and slid the bag back into place, turning to the valley below. He remembered where he had seen the smoke rising from before, and did his best to make a mental note of that direction. Then he reached his hand back into a small pouch on the side of his bag and dug out a compass. It was small, purchased at K-Mart by his dad a few months prior as a requirement for Scouts, but the needle held true north and it did what it needed to. Some of the other kids had gotten really nice survival compasses with all the *fluff*, as his dad had called it. His had the lanyard attachment, direction and degree markings. His dad had told him that he didn't need all that extra stuff. *"You think Lewis and Clark had a fire starter and screwdriver set in their compass? North, east, south and west. That's all you need kiddo. All that other stuff is just fluff."*

His daddy had been right. He could make his own fire, and a screwdriver and level weren't going to help him right now. He eyed where he had seen the strand of smoke rising and gathered his bearings. Then David closed the compass and began his trek down.

A half-hour passed before he reached the bottom. The fresh snow had made everything that much more slippery. Twice the ground beneath him had slid away, sending him four feet down on his butt. By the time he reached the bottom his hands were sore again, the small blister on his left palm burning beneath the glove.

The river crossing was a few yards away and before making his way to it, he stopped and listened, his ears working overtime under his dirty beanie. After a moment he made his way to the river's edge, lifting a heavy rock and dropping it down on the ice at the edge. The rock broke through, the current pulling it a few feet away before it sunk to a stop beneath. Then he leaned down, pressing his lips to the current and drank deeply. A moment later he rose, wiping his mouth on his sleeve and started towards the crossing.

He traversed the rocks carefully. The drop in temperature last night had returned the thin coating of ice layered atop. He stepped one stone at a time, taking time to get his balance centered before moving to the next. A few minutes later he was across and making his way into the trees. He walked a few yards in before stopping. He stood there in thought, his breath clouding in front of him. Then he pulled his compass out and got his bearings once more. Southeast, a hundred and thirty-two degrees. All he had to do was keep aware of his surroundings and check his compass every now and then. He folded the compass and slid it into his pocket, starting forward.

As David made his way through the quiet woods, he checked his compass every so often to make sure he was still headed in the right direction. Each time he would turn and fix his heading. It was about an hour later that the faint smell of campfire wafted past. He stopped, dropping to a knee and scanning the woods beyond. The trees were quiet and he couldn't hear anything other than the soft rustle of his clothes as he shifted slightly. He sniffed. It wasn't smoke he'd smelled, and as he looked up through the trees, he realized there was none rising up. It was the smell that was left when a fire had gone out and only a few embers were left smoldering. It was the smell his cave had every time he crawled back in. He struggled to formulate a plan on what he would do if he found the man, what he *could* do. He wasn't even sure why he wanted to. There was no rescuing his mom, no reason at all to be there. Yet, something told him he had to. He had to see him. There was something he had to be able to do, but he just didn't know what.

He stayed there, knelt to the ground in thought for the next few minutes before rising up and carefully stepping through the snow. Each step he took he paused and listened. It was a few minutes later that he found the source of the smell.

Twenty feet away, in the middle of a small clearing was a campsite. Parked near the single road leading out was an older model pickup truck, orange with a thick white stripe running along its side. There was a tent a short distance from the truck and next to that a single campground style bench table set up with a metal grated firepit.

David could see the thin trail of smoke rising only a few inches up from the pit, a quick indication that the fire had just barely gone out. Sitting atop the grate was a metal coffee pot.

He eyed the camp, his gaze moving to the items resting atop the bench. Then his gaze went wide, his stomach tightening. At the edge of the table was his daddy's backpack. He knew it instantly, without even seeing the Yellowstone patch his daddy had ironed on three years before. He knew it was his. It was black with a dark green trim and had a gold zipper. He could hear his mommy teasing his daddy about his *'fancy new bag'* when he first bought it. Lying next to the bag was an assortment of pots and metal plates. Lying next to those was an open bag of beef jerky and *the knife*.

David tensed, staring at the blade that had killed his mommy and daddy. The handle was burned into his memory; jet black with silver at the base. In an instant his gaze jerked away and he moved behind the trunk of a large pine, pressing his back against it as he stared wide-eyed into the trees. Then a sound froze the blood in his veins, sending waves of panic through him.

A short distance away a loud *cough* rang out. It was deep and wet, like how his had sounded when he had gotten pneumonia two years before. It felt to David like that one time he had been taking a sip of juice and accidentally inhaled a bit of it.

He stood there, listening as another cough sounded out. Then he heard the crunching of feet through the snow just behind the tree.

"Fuckin' snow," the man grumbled as he walked towards camp, pulling his zipper up. "How I always end up getting' caught in this shit? Shoulda bought that fuckin' camper trailer."

The man stepped back into camp, grumbling to himself as he made his way to the table where his coffee cup sat. He reached out, picking it up and bringing it to his lips. He took a sip and then made his way back to the pot, lifting it up and tilting it over his cup. Two drops fell out. Frustrated he set the pot back down on the grate with a clank. Then he set his cup next to it and made his way back to the table. "Alright," he growled, reaching out to pick up David's daddy's backpack. He pulled the contents from within; a rolled-up sweater, a pair of gloves and some socks. Then he pulled out a small pocket knife and a lighter. Beneath was a polaroid photo. The man pulled it out and stared at it for a moment before hissing, *"Fuckin' family man"* and dropping the picture to the ground. He picked up his knife, working it onto his belt. "No more games," he said, pepping himself up as he stretched his head to the side, cracking his neck. "Take care of that little shit and then get the *fuck* out of here. Fuck this snow."

David dropped low behind the tree, pulling his hand into the sleeve of his jacket and bringing it to his mouth. He breathed into the sleeve, concealing both the sound and the sight of his breaths. He knelt there, listening as the man complained to himself. He heard the footsteps draw closer. He tensed as the soft crunching grew, then a moment later the killer stepped into view, making his way into the trees. David edged around the side of the tree as quietly as he could. All the man needed to do was turn his head or look over his shoulder and he would have been caught. But the man kept trudging forward, and in a moment David had slid around the other side of the trunk and out of view.

He rose, ready to bolt, but stood there unmoving for the next few minutes instead. He took a deep breath, forcing himself to relax and gathering his nerve. Another few minutes passed before he built up enough courage to step out from behind the tree. He turned and quickly made his way into the killer's camp.

David darted to his father's bag, opening it quickly and putting his own inside. Then the photo lying in the snow caught his eye. He reached down, picking it up. Three happy faces smiled back. The picture had been taken during the renaissance fair they had in town every year. Mommy had her hair up, a bundle of curls all wrapped up on top and his daddy was wearing a big, pointed green hat with a long feather sticking out towards the back. David had insisted on getting his face painted like a raccoon, so he had a large black band across his eyes and thin whiskers drawn out across his cheeks. For two weeks after his daddy had called him his little trash panda. He still didn't quite understand what that meant, but it made his mommy and daddy smile, so it didn't bother him much.

He stood there, staring at the photo as a barrage of emotions pummeled him. He stared until the pain became overwhelming, and then tore his gaze away, lowering the memory and placing it into in his pocket. He couldn't cry, he wouldn't. Little kids cried and he wasn't a little kid anymore.

David turned his attention to the other items on the table, the half a bag of jerky, some dried fruit, an opened pack of cigarettes and a lighter. He quickly scooped up the jerky and fruit and dropped them into his daddy's bag. His eyes settled on the cigarettes for a moment. He knew they were bad. His mommy and daddy had told them that. But he also knew about 'diction. His grandpa had been 'dicted. It took him ten years, his daddy had said, to quit smoking. He thought about how his daddy had said it.

"He was one irritable bastard."

He knew the killer would be the same. So, he reached out and lifted the pack, pulling the cigarettes out and breaking them into pieces. He let the rolled paper and tobacco fall to the snow beneath, then crushed the red and white cardboard box into his hand and threw it as far as he could. He stood there, the sense of accomplishment warming him for a moment. Then he turned to the truck. The man had popped the tires on his parent's car so that they couldn't escape. He would do the exact same thing. David made his way over and pulled out his knife, unfolding it. As he knelt, a sharp ping of fear worked into him. He'd never popped a tire before and was afraid of what would happen. He'd had a bike tire pop once, and it had been loud. What if the killer heard it and came running back? He knelt there, a multitude of worries all battering him at once. Then in one swift motion he plunged the blade in, puncturing the wall of the tire.

PSSSST!

A loud hiss burst out, the sound evaporating in a second. He stared, watching as the weight of the truck pressed the tire flat. Then he rushed to the next and repeated it. Moments later all four of the truck tires had been punctured. After he finished with the last tire, he made his way to the fire, scooping as much snow from around it as possible to extinguish the remaining embers. He piled the snow up to the grate and then picked up the coffee pot, throwing it as far as he could away from the camp. He took the cup and dropped it into his bag and turned, darting back into the trees. He followed his tracks, running quickly. An hour later he was emerging from the trees at the river's edge. A few minutes after that he was making his way back up the mountainside.

David felt a surge of pride as he crawled into his den and pulled the door back into place. He'd faced his fears and gone down to find the killer. He hadn't known what he was going to do when he did and hadn't thought through the consequences. He just knew that he had to find him. As he moved to the back he smiled, knowing how angry the man was going to be when he got back and saw that his tires had been popped. The man couldn't leave, and his fire was out. He didn't even have a lighter to start it again.

The smile on his face only grew as he reached into his daddy's pack and then into his. He pulled out one of the remaining sandwiches, taking half and setting it on his leg as he refolded the other portion in the plastic and returned it to the bag. The man was going to be so angry when he couldn't make his coffee too. He'd seen his daddy get mad when there was no coffee in the morning because they ran out. He knew the bad man would feel even worse. Wait 'til he gets hungry and his jerky is gone. The thought brought a smile to his face as he lifted the sandwich to his lips.

He sat there with a sense of accomplishment and he ate the half sandwich. Afterwards he pulled a can of soda out and cracked it open. David purposely poured it into the cup and sat smiling as he slowly sipped the fizzy drink. It was still early, mid-day by where the sun sat overhead, but the killer was out looking for him, and he had already accomplished his mission. With that, he decided to use the next part of the day to study his book. Once he was sure he wouldn't be seen, he would go back out and start the following stage of his plan. That involved getting more sticks and building some traps in case the man tried coming up the mountain.

Chapter 24

The campsite was still, the embers in the pit cold and black beneath eight inches of snow. At first glance, nothing seemed to be off. It wasn't until the killer made it ten feet out of the trees that he stopped, a puzzled suspicion making its way across his face. The single thought that had been working his mind was firing up the coffee pot and getting another hot cup in him. That's what caught him. Where the hell was his coffee pot?

He stood there, his gaze working across the small clearing and taking a mental inventory of the site. His coffee pot lay about fifteen feet away, the dark blue spout just visible in the snow. His cup was nowhere to be seen and someone had gone and piled snow into his firepit. The bag was missing from the table along with his jerky and bag of dried peaches. Then his eyes fell to his truck, a moment passing before he registered the smallest change in height as he stared down to the rims sitting flat against the snow beneath.

"You mother...FUCKER!"

His face whipped wildly around the campsite, begging to see the boy.

"You're fucking dead! You hear me!? Fucking DEAD!"

He stormed to where the coffee pot lay, bending down and picking it up angrily. He made his way back to the firepit and slammed the pot down on the grate. "FUCK!"

He turned and started towards his truck, grumbling the whole way. "I'm done," he growled as his face warped into a violent scowl. "No more games. I'm comin' you little piece of shit. I'm gonna rip your fuckin' guts out and dance on 'em."

He circled the truck, a cold realization settling in. The fleeting moment of helplessness only served to fuel the malice burning beneath his skin. Never in his days... He'd had folks talk back and women try to fight him off. He'd been shot at, slashed with a purse knife across the arm, and had a single scar running down the side of his neck just behind the ear, left by an acrylic nail from a hooker outside reno just before she felt his hands around her throat. But never, ever in his life had he ever had some piece of shit kid get under his skin like this. He could feel the rage churning, the embarrassment fanning the flames. How?! How the hell?! What kind of balls did that little fucker think he had?

"I swear to god I'm gonna skin you alive and leave you for the wolves."

The man took a deep breath, cursing under his breath as he made his way back towards the fire, his hands working through his jacket pockets. Then he stopped, his eyes flicking back and forth as his hands began to pat down his pockets feverishly. He stilled, his head slowly turning to where he had left his last pack of cigarettes and the only lighter he had.

"FUUUUUUUCK!"

Chapter 25

Chambers was busy. With Christmas just around the corner everyone was rushing to stock up. Turkey, ham, stuffing mix and cranberries were flying out the door as a mildly frantic group of people made their last-minute preparations. Amongst those people was Jack, the man whom Mike had spoken to just a few days prior, the captain of his bowling league and the same man who carried a deepening concern over his friend not making it to practice the day before.

"That gonna be everything, hon?"

Jack pulled his gaze from the parking lot where he had just watched the sheriff pull in.

"Uh, yeah. Sorry, Jan. I think that'll do her."

"Ya'll got family coming in this year?"

Jack smiled, stealing another quick glance outside. "Not this year. The boy's spending it in California with his girlfriend and her folks."

"Oh!" the cashier replied, surprise rising on her face. "Cody's found himself a girlfriend. That's nice. Is he thinking about settling down?"

"You let me know," Jack smiled.

The cashier returned the grin, quickly glancing at the small screen in front of her. "Welp. That'll run you thirty-six twenty."

Jack smirked, pulling two twenties out of his wallet and handing them over.

The girl returned his change and smiled. "You have yourself a nice Christmas."

"Oh, I reckon you'll be seeing me again before that. You know Mavis always forgets something and sends me right back out."

The girl chuckled. "Well, you tell Mavis I said hello."

"Will do," he replied, picking up the three bags. "And merry Christmas to you."

Jack turned and made his way out, picking up his pace the moment he hit the cement. The sheriff had parked a short distance from him and was just stepping out as he closed the gap.

"Hey, Sheriff," Jack called out, continuing forward. "You got a sec?"

The sheriff closed the door to his truck and nodded. "Sure thing, Jack," he said as the older man walked up. "What can I do you for?"

"I'm a bit worried actually? It's about the Connor family."

"Oh," the sheriff replied, his brow furrowing. "What's on your mind?"

"Well," Jack started, shifting the bags in his hand to get a better grip. "That's the thing. You see, I spoke with Mike the other day and he said they was going out to do that whole tree-cutting thing they do every year." He paused. "Kind of their own little tradition. But, uh, I'm not so sure they made it back."

"Why's that?" The sheriff regarded him quizzically.

"They weren't at church this Sunday, and Mike never made it to our league practice."

"Maybe they took a little vacation."

"Eh," Jack replied with uncertainty. He'd considered that for a split second also, but there was no way Mike wouldn't have told him. And for sure no way he'd miss practice. "Thought crossed my mind. But here's the thing sheriff. Every Monday, like clockwork, for the last five years Mike ain't never missed a single practice. Hell, I don't think even a coma would keep him from missing it. I'm just worried, that's all. Somethin' don't feel right."

The sheriff turned his head, glancing towards the mountains in the distance. "Well. You know how those old back roads can be.

That car of theirs ain't exactly four-wheel drive," he smirked, then paused noticing Jack's genuine unease. "But I suppose it wouldn't hurt none to head out and take a look. On account of the boy being with 'em and all."

"I'd appreciate that, Sheriff. I really would."

"Where'd you say they went again?"

"You know that old logging road off the ninety-four, the one the teenagers like to go have their keg-parties on."

"Yeah," the sheriff replied with a sigh. "I know the one."

"That'd be where."

The sheriff glanced towards the Christmas tree lot a short distance away. "Why don't they just buy their tree like everyone else? Evelyn and I still can't figure that one out."

"Well," Jack replied with a soft smirk. "Traditions are traditions."

"How's Mavis?"

Jack nodded. "She's good. She's uh, she's doing good."

"Ya'll get yours already?" the sheriff asked, nodding towards the tree lot.

"Oh. Reckon I'll pick one up in the next day or so."

"Better do it quick. All the good ones are liable to be gone in the next few days. What about the boy? He gonna be back for Christmas?"

"Nah," Jack answered for the second time that day and probably far from the last. "He's got himself a girlfriend now. Plannin' on spending the holidays with her family."

"Well let's hope he don't make a habit out of it."

"Nah. He's a good kid. His roots are here."

"Well," the sheriff said, glancing down at the bags in Jack's hands. "Suppose I'll let you get to it. I'm gonna grab a few things for myself before it's all gone. I'll shoot out and check on Mike in the morning. You have yourself a good day now. Send Mavis our regards."

"Will do," Jack replied, nodding as he turned. "Merry Christmas."

"Same to you, Jack."

The older man made his way back to his truck, opening the door and sliding his groceries across the bench. He had a bad feeling in his gut, something just sat wrong. Folks had gone missing in the mountains before, but Mike grew up there and he knew those hills like the back of his hand. Something wasn't right, and if he wasn't already pushing seventy, he'd have gotten in his truck and gone out looking himself. He sat there, sight locked onto the thin lines cracked into his steering wheel, the thoughts repeating in his head. He shook them off, stuck the key in the ignition and turned the truck on, backing out and making his way home.

Chapter 26

David had nearly reached the cave when the shadows darkened, the cold pressing downwards and sending a shiver through him. In minutes the temperature had dropped and he went from sweating beneath his jacket to the cold piercing in. He'd gone back out, making his way down the slope to the woods below. He'd filled his belly with water and bundled a few rigid branches together, which he was managing to wrestle back up the ravine. He finished the last part of the ascent and turned, staring back down into the valley. His gaze worked to where the killer's camp had been and he felt the tickle of a smile tugging at his cheeks. He'd got him good. For the next few minutes David stood there feeling the proud sense of accomplishment return. He took joy in knowing how angry the man would be when he found his camp and realized that his fire was out and he couldn't have his coffee or his cigarettes. Most of all, he felt a bitter content knowing that the man couldn't leave either. It meant that they were both stuck there, and that the killer would eventually have to come and find him.

David darted to the two dead trees he'd found and began pulling smaller branches off. He'd gotten the larger ones from below for the main part of the trap. Now he just needed some smaller ones to fill the holes. He spent the next twenty minutes whittling the sticks into sharp points with his knife. With that done, he bundled them up and carried them to where the ravine flattened out. He placed them in a neat pile and set to gathering stones. He stacked them three high, running a length of twine between the first two and connected a series of four. Anyone or thing passing close by would trip the string and send the stones clattering down. He'd have time to hide or get away. Though, at that close distance, he would only be able to run and he hoped he was fast enough to escape.

David bundled the sharp sticks together with twine and hoisted them up, carefully making his way back down and halfway between the plateau and the river's edge. He spent the next hour digging three small pits in the base of the ravine and jammed the sticks in, pointed side up. He covered them with some broken branches. He repeated the string and stone warning system just above. For this one he added the soda can so that it would be extra loud. Satisfied, David turned and made his way back up.

By the time he had finished the sun was already cresting behind the mountain. He'd worked up an appetite and was satisfying the grumbling beneath his coat with a small piece of jerky. He stood there chewing as he looked out across the snow-topped trees. He knew that somewhere down there, the man who killed his parents was hunting him and that he was very angry. For the briefest of moments, he almost felt the worrying clutch of regret. Almost, but not quite. The man deserved it. He was a bad person, and bad people should have bad things happen to them. David wasn't big enough to do anything else, but as his daddy liked to say, he had *leveled the playing field* a bit.

David spent the next few hours studying his book. He read and reread chapters, honing his skills and taking the time to not only learn, but to memorize key lessons. He studied foraging and took note of what plants and berries were edible. He studied the basics of shelter building and how to construct a fireplace inside to keep warm in the winter. He was grateful that he had found the den as that had taken care of much of the problem. It did get really smoky inside with the fire and there were a few times he had needed to move the door aside and fan the smoke out. But it stayed warm, and once the walls collected enough heat, it retained it for a good portion of the night. It was just the smoke and hard floor. The second part he decided to address sooner than later, setting his book down and making his way out to forage for more ground cover and nearby plants to pile as bedding. Then he climbed back in, pulled the door closed and set about prepping his fire. A short time later he was sitting in the warmth of the glow, his book in one hand and half a sandwich in the other.

Chapter 27

The killer had spent the remainder of the afternoon traipsing through the woods in search of the boy. He'd tracked and backtracked, following the trail back to the river and following it up and down for at least a half-mile in each direction. Somehow the little sum' bitch was clever enough to evade him. That only served to piss him off even more. Eventually the cold had set in and he was forced to make his way back to camp. With no lighter and no fire, he was sitting in his truck, the engine running and heater on.

He glanced at the dash. Quarter tank... He'd leave the engine running a while longer before making his way out to his tent. At least the little bastard hadn't gone and sliced that up too.

The man reached down, pulling a small plastic bottle of vodka off the floor and slowly twisted the cap off. He lifted it, taking a deep swig. As he did, something caught his eye, the faintest flicker of light on the side of the mountain. He slowly lowered the bottle, his eyes straining to pick up the glow again. A thin smile slithered across his cheeks as an ember of yellow peered through the clouds.

"Got you."

Chapter 28

The next morning there was a soft rustling, followed by the noise of a zipper being drawn. The sound shattered the quiet still surrounding the killer's camp. The tent flap fell open and a moment later out stepped the man, his messy dark hair falling around his shoulders.

He stood straight, stretching his shoulders back with a groan. He moved the stink in his mouth around with his tongue, the bitter flavor of vodka and heartburn moving past. He reached back into the truck and opened the glove compartment, moving things around for a moment before coming out with a small package of peanuts.

He sniffed, turning his head to the side and covering one nostril as he shot a large ball of snot into the snow at his feet from the other. Then he wiped his nose with his sleeve and ripped the top of the peanut package open.

The bag tore open at a crooked angle, sending half of the contents into the snow below. "Son of a…" he groaned, not bothering to bend down and pick them up. He rolled the remainder up and stuffed them in his pocket, half-crawling back into the truck to grab the last sip of vodka left. He lifted the small plastic bottle to his lips and drained it, sniffling again as he tossed the bottle aside and pulled the peanuts out, chasing the flavor away.

For the next few minutes, he stood there, the slight pressure from the night before lingering behind his eyes. After letting loose a deep exhale he turned his gaze to the mountain.

Chapter 29

Less than a mile away from where the killer stood prepping himself for the coming climb, Sheriff Keith Bowman was pulling off the old ninety-four. He turned onto the single lane road leading in, a road he knew all too well. The local kids liked to come all the way out here to throw their parties. They'd been doing so for generations. But so long as they cleaned up after themselves and didn't cause any problems, he didn't much care. He'd had his own spots just like it as a teen. Nowadays he had other issues to worry about; the main one a growing community that depended on the supply and distribution of methamphetamine that had sprung up over the past few years. On more than one occasion he'd gotten a call about a trailer going up in a ball of flames on the outskirts of town, or one of his deputies finding a trunk full of dope behind out of state plates. So what if some kids had a kegger? Hell, he'd done the same at his age, multiple times, and at the same spot. He pushed the thoughts away and continued down the snow-covered road, his tires crunching beneath.

The gold Town & Country sat under three inches of snow, a strange calm hanging over the macabre scene. The sheriff's truck slowed just at the edge of the turnaround, his tires crunching to a stop. A feeling he was all too familiar with wormed in immediately, one he had come to hate over the years. He sat there for a moment, taking it in. The abandoned car, the tree on top… That's the thing that struck him as odd, the thing that carried the weight of worry. They'd already cut the tree. Why would they put the tree on top and then head back out into the woods? His gaze moved to the ground, to the left, and he felt the blood in his veins ice over. Just twenty feet away, partially covered in snow was what looked to be the blood-covered corpse of Mike Connor.

The door to the sheriff's truck creaked open. He stepped out, the chill outside meeting the one growing within. Instinctively, his hand moved to the small leather strap holding his pistol in place, his finger flicking the snap free as his palm rested on the handle. He started forward.

He stopped just short of Mike's body. He could see the deep, open gash across his neck and the dark stain on his chest where he'd been stabbed. He took it in, his eyes flickering to the woods for a moment before settling back on the frozen corpse. They lingered here a moment longer before turning to the other. He felt a hard lump tighten in his stomach at the sight. His heart skipped a beat, quickening in pace and then pounding heavy in his chest. He felt the gripping fingers of panic clutch at him, and in an instant his mouth became dry. Sheriff Bowman started towards the second body, his eyes taking in the gruesome scene as his hand numbly drew his pistol from its holster. Lying face up in the snow, skin a dull blueish white, was Cheryl Connor. It was obvious by the torn clothing and blood on the inside of her thighs what had happened to the poor woman. His eyes worked across the multiple stab wounds at her chest and then to the gash running across her throat so deep that her spinal cord showed through. His gaze settled on her own, lifeless and dull, eyes wide open and clouded blue.

Sheriff Bowman turned to the side, choking back a sob induced vomit, his back arching as he fought to keep his breakfast in his stomach. His grip tightened on his pistol and scanned the area, struggling to compose himself. His eyes darted around frantically, searching for the third body, but it was just the two, the parents. Where was the boy?

He turned, walking quickly back to his truck, his hands now shaking.

"Dispatch, this is Sheriff Bowman, do you copy?"

He stood there, his gaze locked to the bench seat of the truck, the world around him a hazed blur.

"Dispatch here," a reply came back over the radio. "I read you, Sheriff."

Sheriff Bowman took a deep breath, his eyes drifting back to the bodies of Mike and Cheryl. "I'm uh." He stopped, swallowing hard. "I'm. I'm out off old ninety-four. The logging turnout the kids throw their summer parties at." He paused again, the words forming in his mind feeling strange and foreign. He didn't want to speak them, as if keeping them hidden behind his lips would make it go away. "I uh. I just found the Connor family. They're uh. They're dead. Someone killed them. It's bad."

"Come again, Sheriff?"

"The Connors. They've been murdered."

A moment of silence passed.

"Look, uh. Marie. I need you to call the fellas and get 'em up here as quickly as possible."

"Jesus, Keith," the woman replied. "The whole family?"

Sheriff Bowman looked over the clearing once more. "I don't see the boy, so I'm gonna grab my rifle and head out on foot. Get a call out to Terry and see if we can't get a chopper in the air. We're gonna need all the help we can get on this one. And get a line out to the state."

"I'll get the deputies out ASAP. Is there anyone else you want me to notify?"

"Best get Jim on the line. We're gonna need a wagon." He paused. "And Marie?"

"Yeah, Sheriff?"

"Would you mind giving Evelyn a call for me? Let her know it's gonna be a late night."

"Sure thing, Sheriff."

Sheriff Bowman set the mic back in its cradle and closed the door, stepping back onto the scene. Having had a moment to compose himself, he turned his focus back to the turnaround. It was obvious that they'd been caught off guard, but it didn't make much sense. It wasn't like it was summertime and a bunch of folks were out camping and hunting. It was the dead of winter and there was snow on the ground. Someone must have followed them up. But who, and why? He scanned the ground for tracks, but with the snow that had fallen the last few days it was hard to say which had come and gone. It was a perverted miracle that the Connors' bodies were even exposed.

He stepped closer, his training edging back in. Whoever had done this had gotten to Mike first. It didn't look like there was much of a struggle. Maybe they caught him off guard? Then Cheryl... He tried not to think about it. He'd sat next to them in church, had been at their wedding. He pushed the thoughts away, turning to look at the car. He slowly made his way around and spotted the faint reminder of tracks leading away.

He walked over to the marks and knelt down. They were covered in fresh powder, but the impressions were still there, although barely. Two sets, one obviously the boy, and the other... A size ten boot, male. By the distance he gauged that the boy had left in a sprint, but the man had followed at a walking pace. The sheriff felt his already pounding pulse quicken even more.

Sheriff Bowman stood, his gaze scanning through the trees. He looked over at the mountain peak rising through the tree line in the distance. He reached up with a heavy hand and pulled his hat off, wiping his brow with his sleeve before sliding it back on. He turned and made his way back to his truck.

Opening the camper shell, he pulled his rifle case to him. He opened it and took out his thirty-ought-six. He drew back the bolt, checking that it was loaded, and grabbed a handful of shells and dropped them in his pocket. He slid the rifle strap over his shoulder and pulled a pair of binoculars out of a small box. Sheriff Bowman then closed the shell and turned, making his way back to the tracks.

"Oh, kid…" he whispered, his breaths puffing out. "I'm comin.'"

Chapter 30

At the same time Sheriff Bowman discovered his parents below, David was just opening his eyes. He lay there for a moment, staring at the roof of the den. The temperature had dropped, but the cave had stayed relatively warm. He'd only had to wake up twice to add a few sticks to the fire. David pulled his gaze from the ceiling and turned his head to the side, letting the doorway fall into view. He could see the light coming in from outside and knew it was well into morning. For the next few minutes, he lay there. Finally, with a big yawn, he stretched out his arms and legs, extending them as far as they could go before bringing himself to a seated position.

David lay thinking about the day before, a tingle of satisfaction prickling through. A smile tugged at the edges of his lips as he imagined the man's reaction coming back to find his truck tires popped and his fire out. His dad had told him many times that revenge was never the way to go, that it was never worth it. But as he lay there, thinking about the man screaming in anger, his fists pounding into the snow in frustration and 'diction, he knew that this time had to be different. That man deserved it. He was bad, and he deserved to have bad things happen to him. David knew that his dad would understand. He shook the thoughts off before reaching out slowly to grab his daddy's pack and pulling the lunch bag out. He fished out the last sandwich and unwrapped it, setting one half on his leg and wrapping the other half before placing it back in the bag. He decided to save the last banana and soda for later. He knew he didn't have much longer before he had to figure out what to do for food. He'd seen the fish, so he knew they were there. Maybe he could build a fishing pole out of wood and the twine. He knew you could fashion a hook from the top of a soda can. Maybe he could try that. He sat in silence, pondering his next move as he finished eating the half-sandwich.

The sun was warm across his face when he crawled to the exit and made his way out, even though he could still see his breath. It felt good. He allowed himself a little bit of time to soak it in before unzipping his pants. As he peed, the thin stream arching downwards, he let his eyes work over the valley below. Not long after he'd shaken and zipped back up, a sound rose up the hillside, a sound familiar, distant, but close enough to raise the flesh on his arms as the blood froze in his veins. There was a light clattering of stones accompanied by the tinny tinkle of an aluminum can bouncing down the rocky slope.

David's gaze whipped to the ravine. Already a hundred feet up the mountain and rising quickly was the killer. He'd somehow found him, had crossed the river and was quickly making his way in David's direction. The man looked up, pausing for a moment but not seeing David. Then he dropped his gaze and continued clambering upward.

David spun, rushing back into the cave and crawled as fast as he could to the back. He frantically shoved his book and lunch bag into the backpack and spun, making his way back out in seconds. In an instant he was rushing to the slope and climbing.

Below, the killer continued his ascent. The slope was still slippery from the morning frost and his hands worked to find holds as he crept up. A clatter of stones above caught his ear and he lifted his gaze to see the young boy headed towards the peak. His face dropped into a scowl as he stared, his teeth gritted tightly. He lowered his gaze, a low growl escaping his lips, and pushed himself to move faster.

David climbed as quickly as he could. He knew that once he was at the top, he wouldn't have anywhere to go. But if he tried to go back down, the man would easily beat him to the bottom and would just be there waiting. It would take the killer longer to climb up than to slide back down. So, David chose the longer of the two options and scrambled for the peak.

He had climbed about fifty feet when a rock pulled free and his hand slipped. He felt gravity yank him down and he slid about ten feet back before his leg caught on a root and stopped his descent. He jerked his gaze back down the mountain to see the killer still advancing. He had to keep going, no matter what. With sharp breaths, he turned his focus back to climbing.

Not long passed before the killer reached the halfway mark between the bottom and the first outcropping. He brought his foot up and felt it catch against something. A pile of rocks clattered down the slope behind him. He looked down to see another strand of twine wrapped around his foot and bent to pluck it free. He turned his gaze back to the boy to find the kid had nearly reached the top. *Fuckin' kid is fast*, he thought, grumbling as he continued up. His lungs were burning and he could feel the angered bite of irritation he knew all too well snapping at him. It'd been over twelve hours since his last smoke. The thought angered him even more.

He had made it another ten feet when he crawled past the branches laid out. He moved to take another step when his foot landed on the pile. The branches there instantly gave way and his foot dropped down into the hole. He felt a blinding pain as three sharpened sticks plunged into his calf.

David heard the scream from above and turned, peering back down the slope to where the killer was. He could see him yanking his leg from the hole and watched as the man continued to yell. He couldn't make out what the killer was saying, but he could see the blood coming from his leg. His trap had worked!

Back in the woods below the Sheriff Bowman heard a distant scream echo out. He moved to a spot where he could get a clear view of the mountain and raised the binoculars to his eyes. He scanned the slope, starting at the top and working his way down. Then he spotted the boy. He could see David scrambling to reach the top, rocks dropping free and rolling downward behind as he struggled to find handholds. Sheriff Bowman traced the line of sight further down. Halfway up the mountain was another figure following in chase.

Sheriff Bowman adjusted the binoculars, twisting the small dial at the top and zooming closer. He could see blood on the man's leg, but he wasn't stopping. He needed to get to the boy and fast, so he lowered the binoculars, unslung his rifle, and started running as fast as he could through the trees.

The killer climbed the next twenty feet in agony. There were two deep gashes in his leg and a puncture wound that ran against the bone. He could feel the blood filling his boot, but he didn't stop. Only a single thought pounded his head.

"I'm gonna kill you!" he screamed, lifting his gaze to the boy a hundred yards away. "I'm gonna throw you off this FUCKING MOUNTAIN!"

David heard the man's yell, pausing only long enough to gauge his distance. He turned and scrambled towards the peak twenty feet away. In moments he was pulling himself to the flat area on top. He whipped his gaze back and forth, looking for an escape. He was frantic, but tried desperately to keep his thoughts together. *"It's when you rush that you make mistakes. Measure twice, cut once,"* his father's words echoed in his head.

David knew that one side had the sheer cliff dropping to the valley below, and the other only took him further up, but the slope on the backside was far too steep to descend. He had two options, make his way further up and try to slide down past the rapidly approaching killer, or make his way down towards the ledge and hide behind the fallen tree. He stood there, thinking, trying his best not to let his panic take over. Maybe he could buy himself enough time for the killer to think he went down the other side. If the man was hurt, he might be able to run past him and slide back down. If he could get back to the woods below, he could run to where his mommy and daddy's car was, and he could follow the road from there. He knew the town was a long distance away, but he still had the half a sandwich and a banana. Plus, the man's leg was hurt really bad, so it would be hard for him to follow. He might be able to outrun him. David just needed to get past him and back down to the bottom.

He stood there for the next few breaths, cursing himself for not waiting. If he had just waited, the man would have fallen into his trap, and he could have slid down on the other side of the ravine. *Stupid*, he cursed. He should have just waited.

Below, the man had continued his ascent, though the going was much slower with one leg badly damaged. There was a thick trail of blood following behind and he was relying mostly on the strength of his hands pulling him up. His leg pulsed wetly. He went over and over the different ways he was going to kill the boy, the kinds of pain he was going to inflict before he allowed him to die. A kaleidoscope of violent deaths awaited that little bastard once he got his hands on him.

Above, David slid carefully down the slope towards the fallen tree. He made sure not to go too fast. He knew what was on the other side, and if he accidentally knocked the tree over he'd be stuck with nowhere to hide and the cliff to his back. So, even though he knew the bad man was only a short way behind, he kept his pace down the arduous slope deliberate and unhurried. *Slow and steady wins the race.*

The last few feet were a scary, uncontrolled slide that ended against the log. David skid down on his butt, using his feet to stop his momentum once he reached the bottom. He very carefully climbed over the fallen tree, his eyes falling to the dizzying drop off just four feet away. He edged back against the log, taking one last look up the slope. He could hear the small rocks clattering down the other side where the killer was, almost at the top. David dropped down, pressing himself as low as he could behind the log.

Overhead the sky had darkened. The clouds hanging just out of reach shifted from grey to slate. A cold moisture hung in the air and moved leisurely on the breath of a small wind. The sound of air rising up the slope whispered past, a small clattering sound not far behind as the killer's boots kicked away a tiny cluster or rocks jutting out.

A moment later the first hand reached the top, followed by a second. The killer lifted himself up, his leg buckling slightly under the weight. "Ah, fuck!" he yelped, shifting his weight to the other leg. "Where did you go you little shit?" he growled, his eyes in a frenzy and they searched back and forth. There were only three ways he could have gone, and he didn't see the boy standing at the top.

He cursed again, starting forward towards the opposite slope, stopping at the edge twenty feet away. He peered down the steadily sloped drop. It was far too steep to make it down without tumbling, and he could see all the way to the bottom. Only a scattering of hillside brush and loose stones dotted the slope. Not here. He turned, his gaze slithering towards the fallen tree below.

The killer took two steps before the stabbing pain shot up his leg again and he stumbled, falling to one knee. He growled, pulling his knife free. "Oh, I'm gonna cut you boy. I'm gonna cut you slow." He slowly lifted himself to his feet. "You're gonna *beg* me to kill you by the time I'm done." He started forward. "But I ain't gonna do that, no. I wanna watch your skinless corpse tumble down this mountain." He paused, his eyes working the slope down. "YOU HEAR THAT BOY?!"

Behind the tree David pressed further down. His gaze was locked to the ground and his heart pounded heavily in his ears.

The man started forward. "You think what I did to your momma and daddy was something? You just wait and see what I can *really* do."

The killer stopped where the slope of the peak led down. Behind him he heard a clatter of rocks fall loose and tumble down. He turned his gaze, staring suspiciously for a moment before snapping his attention back to the descent where the tree lay. A flash of blue caught his eye and he narrowed his gaze to the spot where the boy's jacket showed, just on the other side of the log. A sickly smile spread across his face and he felt the anxious tingle prickling at the tips of his fingers.

He lowered himself to a seated position and began scooching forward. Little by little he made his way down.

Behind the log David tensed, frozen in fear.

The last little bit of movement sent blinding flashes of pain into the man's leg and there was a moment where he thought he was going to scream out, but he bit into it, forcing the scream down with gritted teeth.

"You thought you was clever, didn't you boy?" the man growled as he drew closer. "But you don't know who you're fucking with. You have *no* idea what happens to people who fuck with me. But you sure as hell is about to find out." The man dropped another five feet before another flash of pain ripped through his leg. His mouth opened wide in a soundless scream. He was aware the boy knew he was right there, and he wanted to see the look on his face when he—

"Argh!"

David screamed as a tight grip grabbed ahold of the hood on his jacket, yanking him upward.

"No more runnin' now boy!" the killer shouted, his foul breath blasting David in the face.

David screamed again, wrestling to get free, but the jacket was zipped up, the tiny strings at the bottom still tightly drawn from the night before. He swung out, twisting and fighting, but the killer's hold didn't falter.

"Fight all you want, you little fucker," the man spat, holding tightly as the boy writhed in his grasp. "That shit ain't gonna do you no good. It's just you and me now."

The killer held tightly, enjoying the feel of the struggling boy. He looked past the kid to the open sky beyond. "You ever wish you could fly?" he asked, his grip tightening around the handle of his knife.

"Sheriff's department, drop the knife! NOW!"

The killer's eyes pressed closed as his lips pulled back into a silent snarl. David watched as his face morphed.

"Drop the knife!" the Sheriff Bowman repeated. "Do it now!"

The killer opened his eyes, staring past David's and deep into his soul. He could feel the grip on his jacket tightening and heard cloth *squeak* beneath the steel grasp.

"Let the boy go and turn around slowly," the sheriff continued.

For a moment David saw the man's gaze flicker past him to the cliff behind. Then he felt the grip on his jacket loosen.

"Just let him go," Bowman ordered, his tone bordering a plea.

The killer leaned closer, the warmth from his breath washing sickeningly across David's face. "We ain't done," he whispered, shoving David ever-so-slightly as he released his grasp and slowly turned to face the sheriff.

David took one step back, his head whipping to judge his spacing behind. He gradually began to edge his way to the side, taking each step as gingerly and quietly as his boots would allow. Standing at the top of the small incline was Sheriff Bowman from town. He had a rifle, just like the one his daddy had, and it was pointed right at the killer.

"Now you go ahead and set that knife down real nice and slow. Then you go on and make your way up to me."

The killer stared back with a squint, something flashing through his eyes. "Well, that's gon' be kinda hard on account a what this here boy done did to my leg. I was just showing him it ain't nice to hurt people you don't know."

In the distance, the faint thrum of helicopter blades could be heard.

"Well, you didn't have much of a problem chasing him up this mountainside, did you? I know 'cause I followed that trail of yours the entire way up."

A thin smile flashed across the killer's face.

"Now I don't much like repeating myself," Sheriff Bowman continued. "So, you go on and put that knife you got down, and make your way back up here real slow-like."

"I don't think that's gon' work out too well for me, on account a what I done to this boy's folks, which I assume you done already saw." A sneer flickered on his face. "Matter a fact, I think you're just as liable to shoot me if I move."

Sheriff Bowman's gaze twitched almost imperceptibly to David who had managed to edge a few feet to the side. "What happens to you is for a judge to decide," Sheriff Bowman said, locking his gaze back on the man. "I'm just here to see that that boy gets home safe and that nobody else gets hurt."

The killer stared up at him, a sour feeling of hatred and defeat twisting his stomach.

"You just come on up," Sheriff Bowman continued, allowing David a few more precious moments to get clear. "I'll take you in and we can talk about everything when we get back to town."

The helicopter drew nearer. It was moving over the valley and headed rapidly in their direction.

The man stared back, a sour realization setting in. He'd had a good run... "Nah," he replied with a sneer. "That just ain't gon' work."

In a flash the killer spun, slashing his knife out at the space the boy had just been. It should've been a clean swipe, right across his neck, ensuring that at least he didn't go out alone, and that the kid got his just dues, but the blade slashed through open air.

For the next moment the killer stood confused, his eyes lost in the empty space. His gaze shifted to the side, locking onto the boy who stood five feet away.

Just behind, the helicopter rose up over the cliff, the blades thundering as wind blasted dust and debris out. David shied further away, watching a flicker of violence flash through the killer's eyes as he lunged forward.

A single gunshot rang out and the killer pitched sideways, the knife dropping from his grasp as he spun backwards and plummeted off the cliff. The air rushed past as the man fell three hundred feet down the jagged drop. His body impacted against an outcropping, a spray of blood erupting from his body as it shattered against the stone. His limp frame tumbled outwards, dropping the rest of the way to the mound of rubble beneath, where it splattered wetly onto a massive boulder before coming to a stop. Overhead the helicopter continued to circle, a single rifle aimed from the passenger side at the still body below.

David stared into the depth in horror, waiting for a hand to come jutting up from below. At no sign of movement, he turned to see Sheriff Bowman carefully make his way down the slope in his direction. David scrambled over the log and crashed into the outstretched arms of the sheriff who had only just reached the bottom. It was over.

Sheriff Bowman signaled to the chopper, pointing down into the valley. A moment later it turned and banked away, disappearing behind the slope. After a few minutes, he gently untangled David's arms from him and held the boy back at arm's length to look him over, scanning for any serious injury.

David trembled fiercely as the adrenaline receded and *everything* that had happened these past few days crashed into him all at once. "My parents..."

"I know son," Sheriff Bowman said softly. "It's okay. It's over." He watched as a stream of tears began to pour onto the young boy's cheeks. He couldn't image the horrors this brave boy had suffered through. "I have no idea how you managed to survive this long. When you're ready, I'll be waiting to hear all about it over a big cup of hot chocolate." His hands squeezed tightly against David's shoulders as he watched the boy's tears continue to fall. He tried his best to smile soothingly, the way Evelyn always does so well, though he doubts it'll do much at all against what this boy had been through. Still, he wanted to make sure David knew that he was safe now, at the very least. "Now, how about we get you home?"